Stories of a Cabin

Lake Superior
Deb Vande Voort

LAKE PEARLS PRESS

ISBN 979-8-999-3241-0-8 Hardcover
ISBN 979-8-9993241-1-5 Paperback
ISBN 979-8-999-3241-2-2 Epub

Copyright © 2025 by Deb Vande Voort
Lake Pearls Press, LLC
www.lakepearlspress.com

Apparently, you can make this stuff up

Contents

Prologue

An out of breath teenage girl dropped her bicycle in the driveway and ran in the house, barely stopping for the screen door. "They're going to tear it down! I just overheard Papa tell the contractor it wasn't worth saving!"

The girl's sister, Ingrid, was in the middle of helping her mother can vegetables. Untying her apron as quickly as she could, she looked to their mother for support. "But they can't tear it down; it's the best one!"

"You had better get there quickly, or it'll be gone soon enough. Go ahead and take the car."

Mattias was a shrewd businessman. The son of a Swedish immigrant, he learned to build homes from his father. His business had grown so much, that he was able to make a very good deal on a piece of land and create a small resort for his eldest daughter as a wedding gift. He could not be more proud.

Today was going to be productive. Trees were being felled, and supplies were being delivered. The newlyweds would have a solid start to their new life, and he trusted Kristofer and Ingrid to make it all work.

As the chainsaws paused, he heard a familiar voice, "Papa! Hej, Papa!"

"TIIIMMMMBBERRR!"

Behind him in the distance, the creak of a large pine tree was followed by a snapping noise and a thud he could feel in his stomach. A swarm of men began taking off branches and dividing the trunk in a cacophony of progress.

As she approached her father, he saw the panicked look on her face. Worried, he asked, "What is it?"

"You can't tear it down!"

"Tear what down?"

"The cabin."

"The old one?"

"Yes. Papa, please, I really want to keep it."

"But it is old, and look at that roof! There are holes in it. It will not be like the nice modern cabins we are building."

"But it means a lot to me, Papa. You know how I love old things, and I am sure this cabin has many good stories."

Mattias sighed. "That will be more work for Kristofer to take care of, have you thought of that?"

"Please, Papa."

The look on her face was softening his resolve, but he knew how much work the upkeep would be. He decided this would best be settled by the man who would be her partner. "Let us ask Kristofer."

"We could just add a bathroom and a bedroom, and repair the roof. The walls are still in decent shape," the younger man offered, watching his bride's face light up as he spoke.

"Ok," agreed Mattias, sighing; "but this will be your work. I will finish the other cabins, and I will give you the budget for the one we would have built in its place. The two of you must figure out how to get it done, yes?"

"Yes!" the couple agreed in unison.

"Go back home and help your mother," he told his daughter. "This man has work to do, and you are keeping him from it!"

"Thank you, Papa! Thank you so much!"

Her hug of delight was all he needed for justifying the decision. "Well...it is your future, it should make you happy," he said.

Circle Tour

"**A**dd that to the death napkin."

Marcia grabbed the carefully folded napkin out of her purse. The 'death napkin' was christened as such the night before when discussing, for the who-knows-how-many'ith-time, what should happen upon her husband's death outside of their wills.

Standing up and holding the napkin as if it held a royal decree, she announced, "It is on the death napkin. It is so written, it will be so done." She then sat, leaned forward and whispered, "Unless, of course, it rains, and I can no longer read it."

"Then take a picture of it," Bill replied flatly, not looking away from his laptop screen.

"What if the rain ruins my phone?"

"Don't be ridiculous."

"We've been planning this trip for years, and all you've been wanting to talk about is dying. Your retirement party was two weeks ago. Unless there's something you're hiding from me, you should be years from being dead. Which of us is actually being ridiculous?"

She knew the look he was giving her. He was either annoyed at her point, or the fact that she was right. She held his gaze, not backing down.

"Our investments are down, and there's talk of a recession. I should have worked longer, just to make sure."

"Are you afraid we'll go hungry?"

"There's a certain lifestyle to which you have become accustomed."

Ugh! He can't be serious. This wasn't about how much they spent, and she knew it. Other than an occasional splurge, they were both pretty conservative with their money. This was about his coming to terms with the idea that he was no longer working. No more spreadsheets, no more emails full of things only he could fix, and no more people clamoring for him to make decisions. His life's work was now in the hands of a much younger man, and he needed to find a new purpose in life.

Marcia took a deep breath and decided to do the breakfast dishes, hoping he wouldn't want to help. He didn't seem to notice as she brought them to the counter and started filling the sink.

This was the beginning of their road trip around Lake Superior, an adventure to both celebrate his freedom and to plan the rest of their lives. They reserved four days at the cabin, to see and do what they could in the area before moving along. So far, they've had dinner with the death napkin and breakfast with retirement regret. Neither were on her list.

The warm water on her hands was comforting as she mindfully scrubbed the last of the egg yolk off her plate. She was determined to be patient with Bill, knowing she'd gone through a similar transition once the last kid left the house.

"What's on our list for today again?" she asked, hoping to direct their thoughts to the more positive here-and-now.

"We've got reservations for a cruise at 10am. Then lunch, then a shipwreck tour. I was just looking at the website for that. It says here that they have sunken ships built before the Civil War for us to see...and oh, it also says there are Bald Eagles along the shoreline."

"That sounds interesting. I mean, the natural stuff is my favorite, but it sounds like some good stories are hidden down there."

"That's what I was thinking, too." He looked up from the laptop at her and frowned. "I should probably be helping you with that," he admitted.

"No need. They can air dry and I'm already done."

"Hmpf."

Yep, needs more to do, she thought.

He sat next to her with his arm around her shoulders as they moved through the water. The warm sun on her face offset the cool breeze coming down from the north, and the smell of the water felt cleansing. Even when she closed her eyes, it was beautiful.

As the captain spoke of the minerals layered through the sandstone, she started to finally feel like they were on vacation. She wondered if Bill could put off his existential crisis until the trip was done. She searched his face for the answer. He was relaxed, taking in the weathered East Channel Lighthouse. She smiled as his countenance responded to the captain's explanation of its history. At least for now, he was enjoying himself, which relieved her anxiety. Over the last few weeks especially, she'd allowed herself the burden of caring a little too much for his emotional state. Perhaps she, too, was adjusting to the unknown ahead.

He caught her watching him instead of the view beyond him, and gave her a wink. She smiled and went back to focusing on enjoying the scenery.

The day came and went in a flurry of details. Shipping lanes, natural wonders, and the history of the region were all covered as parts of the tours. Their tanned faces were smiling as they got back in the car. *This is what we've been working toward*, she thought.

Bill's face shifted as he started the car. "Maybe we should just go back to the cabin and have sandwiches."

"What? Why?" Her annoyance at their short-lived enjoyment could be heard in her voice, though subtly. "Are you really that worried about having enough?"

"Well, ah, no...no, I guess not." He grabbed the steering wheel, using it to reposition himself. "I guess it's just a matter of adjusting to the idea of not having any more paychecks coming in."

"We have other sources of income. We planned well, even our investment lady said so. We're going to be ok."

"I hope so," he muttered, as he pulled the car forward into traffic. "Let's find dinner. Which restaurant would you like to try tonight?"

"I'd like to drive along the lake shore, maybe check out something in Marquette, if you don't mind."

"Sounds like a plan."

"Welcome," said their server, a spunky young man who seemed overly eager to please. "Can I get you something to drink?"

"We'll just have water, thanks," Bill said.

"No problem, I'll be right back with those." He cheerfully disappeared and left them to peruse the menu.

Marcia scowled. "Since when do I not order for myself?"

Bill looked up from the menu, surprised by her question. "What do you mean?"

"You just ordered me water without consulting me."

"Did I?"

She leaned forward, putting her arms on the table. "What has gotten into you? I thought you were looking forward to this trip."

He shook his head as if to reset his focus. "I don't know, I'm sorry. I guess I'm just distracted."

"By what? There's nothing in your life right now except me and this vacation."

"That's not true."

The server seemed to pop up out of nowhere, interrupting the conversation. Setting down their waters before them, he asked, "Are you ready to order?"

Neither were ready, but Marcia was determined to decide for herself what she'd have and didn't take the chance on waiting. "I'll take the BLT and fries. Oh, and a cola please."

"And I'll have the brisket sandwich."

Once the server again disappeared, the silence was like a dense fog, permeating and intrusive. Should she pretend it didn't happen and try to enjoy their evening, or demand answers?

Before she could come to a conclusion, he took a deep breath and began. "Marcia, I probably should tell you..."

He was interrupted by a text. Looking at his phone, the color drained from his face. "I have to take this. I'll be right back." He got up from the booth and walked outside.

The salad course came and went. Their server then brought the entrees, with no sign of Bill.

"Would you like me to keep this under the heat lamp until he comes back?"

"No, it should be okay. He'll be back any moment." She checked her phone to see if he messaged her. Nothing. Deciding to investigate, she pulled up their main investment account. Nothing odd there. The housing market was stable, so that investment was good...what else could it be that worried him so? Was he still worried about how things were going at the Bank?

As she took the first bite of her sandwich, Bill came back and stood at the end of the table, his eyes cast downward, looking for a way to say what he needed to say.

Marcia's concern for his well-being now overshadowed her concern for whatever he'd been hiding. "Please, sit down and tell me what is wrong."

He slid into the booth, remaining at an angle that allowed him to get back out again quickly. "Do you remember me talking about a loan I had to turn down for a restaurant?"

"Well, you didn't tell me the details, but I remember it bothered you."

"Because this no longer involves the bank, but does involve you, I can tell you more details now. I believed in this guy, knew him in school. He had a hard time at life, but he was a hard worker and an amazing chef. He had this girlfriend with a head for business. Seemed like a great couple. He came into a once-in-a-lifetime opportunity to become an owner. The problem was his timing. His credit rating was low due to some health issues in the past, and he was still working to restore his credit." Bill lifted his eyes to match her gaze. "I mean, this guy was repaying stuff that had been written off, he's that conscientious. The only reason he was denied was an algorithm."

"How much did you invest, and where did you get the money? Our investments don't show any change over the past few months. I checked."

"I'll get to that, just let me finish. After the Loan Department denied him, he tried a few more times with other banks. Each time, it cut his credit rating more. It ate at me, and I had no authority to override the determination."

"How's your food?"

The couple stared at their server, confused by his innate sense of bad timing. "Could we get this to go?" Marcia asked, knowing they needed more privacy.

"Sure thing, be right back." He bounded off toward the kitchen, blissfully unaware of the annoyance he was causing.

"Bring the check, too," Bill called out after him.

On the way back to the cabin, they found a scenic spot along Highway 28 to pull over and finish their meal in peace. The view of the lake before them was only impeded by a few bug splats on the windshield, which became more smeared with Bill's efforts to clean them off before turning off the car. As they stared at the water, the bug splats seemed to disappear.

Bill grunted at his sandwich. It was now cold, but still edible. He pulled a piece of meat out and tried it. "Needs more cayenne, and a little more time on the grill," he grumbled. He closed the lid of the container and put it on the dash, disappointed.

"Please continue the conversation," Marcia encouraged, nibbling on her fries.

"Ok, where was I?"

"You felt bad for this guy. What's his name again?"

"Oh yeah. Ah, Elden. Anyway, I arranged for a few private investors to meet with him, and we pulled together and loaned him the money."

"Oh wait! I remember his name. We talked about it, and decided to cash out some other investments. To be honest, I was so busy with my sick mom at the time, I'd forgotten we even did that."

He traced his hands along the steering wheel, focusing intently on the curvature. "We did, and you told me you trusted my judgement."

"And I do."

"Well, maybe that was a problem."

"What happened, Bill?"

His hands stopped. He turned to face her. "The girlfriend. She siphoned it all from him...from us."

"How much were we in for? I forget."

"Fifty thousand. The restaurant will need to go up for sale, but I don't think we're getting our money back."

Marcia decided to delay her reaction to the amount until she had the whole story. "What was she doing with the money?"

"We don't know yet, but there are rumors of gambling debts."

"So, it's gone...No hope of recovery?"

"Right. She hasn't been paying the bills. Even worse, she kept a second set of books to show him, us, and the IRS. The police are involved, and we can't talk about this with our friends and family, it has to stay between us until it blows over. Suffice it to say, Elden is beside himself. He was working night and day to get this thing going, and she was blowing it while he worked."

"That poor man!"

"Honestly, I know it's a lot of money for us to lose, but I'm more worried about him. I wouldn't want this to happen to anyone, but this guy deserved to make a go of it. I've never met anyone who worked so hard, but who had so much stacked against his success. I'm worried he may lose his mind."

Marcia looked down at her sandwich, which was growing less and less appetizing as they spoke. Like her husband, she closed her container and tossed it on the dash of the car. "This was money we invested how long ago?"

"The restaurant opened about five years ago. We were starting to get suspicious because he should have been turning a profit by now. The reviews are excellent, and it's been quite busy. We had an auditor come in, which is how we found out. I can't go into more detail right now because they're still investigating, but it looks like a pretty solid case." He put his arms on the steering wheel, and leaned forward, his head landing on his hands at the top. "Do you know how long I'd been working before I could make that much in a year's time?"

Marcia slid her hand down his spine and back up, resting it just below his neck. "It is a lot of money, but it's not absolute financial destruction for us. We won't go hungry, and we won't have to sell our home." As she said the words, she realized she may be wrong. "Wait. As investors, we're not responsible for the debts of the business, right?"

He leaned back, a look of relief on his face. "No, we made sure our liability ended with the investment. I guess we did something right there."

"You did a lot right. You weren't – no, WE weren't wrong in loaning him the money, nor were the other investors. No one can predict everything that could go wrong with a business, you know that. In fact, you've helped people through unexpected losses like this."

"Yeah, I know, but if I hadn't been the one to pull it all together for him, this wouldn't have happened. I should have known better. I should have protected us better."

"How? How could you have known better? No one could. This wasn't you, this was her. Maybe there's a way for her to pay it back?"

"No, there isn't. There were a number of investors, some who will have lost more. It would take multiple lifetimes to pay that back. Roger's one of the bigger investors on this one. He's doing some wheeling and dealing to see if he can recover anything from the assets. If we get anything, it'll be a pittance, and it'll take a long time." Sliding the seat back to give himself more leg room, he continued. "Even with all our planning and saving, that's still a lot."

"It is, but we still have much more than we did when we started out, right?"

His smirk made her forget for a moment that they were in a serious conversation. "It's a truth universally acknowledged, that a capable man with a good wife must be in want of a fortune."

She looked at him, stunned. Going over his words in her head, it took a moment to separate his meaning from the meaning of the original quote. "How long did it take you to come up with that?"

"It's been my investment motto since you first made me watch the movie."

"I thought you loved Pride and Prejudice!"

"I did, but not in the opening line. It took a few scenes before I saw the humor in it."

"So, you've been holding onto that amazing rewrite for 20 years?"

Bill shrugged. "I thought it was corny."

"I'm — are you kidding me? First, you drop this *minor* problem you've been all emotionally constipated about, and now you tell me you've been holding one of the greatest romantic lines in history in your head? I'm not sure which one upsets me more."

Her pretense of offense included, but was not limited to, crossing her arms and rolling her eyes. The deep sigh was for good measure.

He chuckled as he turned on the ignition and rolled his window down part of the way, letting out some of the heat and humidity building up in the car.

The feel of the fresh lake air in her lungs made her toes long for the sand. "Maybe we should get our minds off of the money. How about we go for a walk on the beach?"

The beautiful surroundings lured them back into vacation mode, and they were again able to live in the moment. A blanket from the car provided a spot to watch the sun melt into the horizon. They talked of their future, the kids, and how the bank would be faring without his leadership. They were finding a balance in dealing with the situation, each finding respite in the feeling of sand under them as they talked. To their dismay, the stars took their rightful place in the night sky, bringing with them a need to put their shoes back on. The fireplace at the cabin seemed a reasonable place to hide from the chill.

"Gin," she exclaimed, laying her cards down on the coffee table.

"You smoked me!"

"You gave me the ten I needed, blame yourself."

His phone rang, sending a line of tension through the muscles in his back. He decided to let the call go to voicemail and continue playing cards in front of the fire.

"Aren't you going to answer that?"

"I don't want to know."

"You won't sleep not knowing, and if you don't sleep, I don't sleep."

"Fine, you deal the next hand then." He slid the cards toward her as he got up and took the call.

"Hey, Roger, what's going on?"

Roger, never a quiet talker, was loud and clear. As Marcia shuffled, she could hear both sides of the conversation.

"As it turns out, Jones is quite the foodie, and he and Elden have become friends. He's so sure Elden had nothing to do with what happened, he's willing to buy the business."

"Are you kidding me?"

"No, but wait — there are contingencies."

Bill stood up and began pacing. "What contingencies? And what are the numbers?"

The pacing kept Marcia from hearing Roger's part of the conversation as Bill paced away from her. She kept her gaze on him, trying to decipher whether the news was good or bad.

Bill turned to walk toward Marcia. As he got close to her, he stopped suddenly. His eyes widened in surprise. "What are we supposed to do with a food truck!?!"

Marcia could hear the rest.

"Jones doesn't want to deal with it. He's got lawyers working out details. This would be his way of buying out what is left of your share after the assets are assessed and the losses calculated. Of course, we have to go through some red tape to make it all legal, and who knows how long that will take. Apparently, the IRS will take its share from the sale of the building and the business itself."

"Let me think about it."

"Honestly, Bill, this is the only way you're getting anything back. Take it or leave it. The numbers aren't good, and there are plenty of restaurants that go under with better numbers."

"Well, then, I guess I have to take it. Can you send me pictures and the information I need to put it up for sale?"

"Before I called, I had it looked over by a friend of mine who used to have a similar one. He sent me an email with all kinds of info. I can send that over. Should help you sell it. Elden's been doing anything he can to pay back whatever he can, as fast as he can."

"Is there anything we can do for him? This must be devastating."

"Like I said, Jones and he have become friends. You know how hard it is to be friends with Jones. Business associates, yeah, but friends? He's pretty closely guarded. Turns out he's had some bad relationships, too, so he's got a soft spot for the situation. He's buying the restaurant and hiring Eldon as the head chef. He's got an accounting firm he trusts to run the money part. Been with him for years. He figures with Eldon's skills and his resources, they could create a higher-end experience. Talk about making honey from dog poop!"

"That's the dumbest metaphor I've ever heard."

"Fits, though."

Bill laughed. "Yeah, you're right, it does. I'll give you this one. Send me the info, I'll break the news to Marcia."

Closing his phone, Bill grinned and shook his head. "You're not going to believe this, but Jones is making honey from dog poop."

"You're right," replied Marcia, "that's one of Roger's dumbest ones."

"We should add a jar of honey for him to the death napkin."

As they were packing up to leave for the next leg of their journey, the email came through on Bill's phone. Marcia zipped her suitcase closed and came over to see the pictures. "That's in a lot better shape than I imagined."

"Yeah, I've not really kept up with what was going on in the business once there were other investors involved. This looks...like we may not have lost so much after all. He kept scrolling through the information as she went to wash up the few dishes from their breakfast.

"I should probably help you with that," he said, putting the phone down.

She remembered when they recently had a similar conversation, and her conclusion at that time. *He needs more to do.* How could a thought be so mundane just a couple of days ago, and now be the answer they were looking for?

She rinsed a plate and handed it to him for drying. "So, I was thinking…"

"Yeah?"

"There's more than one way to get our investment back."

He waited for her to continue, but she didn't. As he grabbed a wet plate and began drying it, he lifted his eyes to meet her gaze.

She had turned fully toward him, cocked her head to the side, and was waiting for him to come up with the answer swimming in her head.

He hated when she did that. How was he supposed to know what she was….*oh, found it!* He dismissed it immediately, saying, "I thought you wanted to spend more time together."

"The two are not mutually exclusive. You love cooking, and you're really good at it. We could put a fan blowing the smell out the window for passersby. They couldn't possibly keep going without a taste."

"Ok, so let's just run with this, see where it goes. What if we used it during local festivals and whatnot? I mean, there's got to be money in it, or there wouldn't be so many of them, right?" The last of the dishes dried and put in the cupboard, he draped the drying towel over a drawer handle.

"And we could sell it when we get sick of it. I doubt we would lose much in depreciation before we knew if we liked it. In the meantime, it'd be an adventure. We could even have the kids help us here and there if they want to make a little extra money. The paint job can't be that much of an investment, considering we already own the truck."

"We may need to update the death napkin," he said, moving their suitcases near the door.

Tired of planning the minutiae of his demise, she pulled the fragile paper from her purse and placed it on the table. Bending her ear to it and standing up again, she feigned shock. A few over-exaggerated chest compressions and mouth-to-mouth breaths later, she checked her watch and hung her head. "I declare the death napkin dead. 8:43 am, July 23rd." She wadded it up and forcefully threw it in the garbage can.

Bill's incredulous look gave way to a small upturned smile. "It probably had it comin'."

"And I'd do it again."

"Maybe we need a life napkin?"

"Life would need a book." Marcia said.

"Oh, hey, speaking of books, we should sign this guestbook before we leave. You know, make our mark on history and all..." Knowing her hand-writing was better than his, Bill handed her the book.

Name: Marcia and Bill
From: Rockford, IL
Highlight: Surprise beginnings

The Goodest Boy

"That looks like our cabin, Boss Man."

Riding shotgun in Chris' old Ford pickup was an 11-year-old English Bulldog recently adopted after the death of his owner. On his face was a crooked underbite and the permanent frown that defined his breed. The couple of missing teeth in his smile made him look less like the protector he once was and more like an old man who found his sense of humor.

Boss Man could no longer jump down from the truck seat, so had to wait for Chris to walk around and lower him to the ground. Once there, he was perfectly capable of keeping up with his new owner, following him into the cabin. He took a sniff around, his nose doing all the work at first but the rest of him eagerly following its lead.

After unloading the truck, Chris decided to take a look around the resort. "Should we go for a walk, Boss?"

Boss Man's nose was in full overdrive as they walked the winding path through the small resort and down to the lake. This, of course, led to a dotted trail of slobber mapping out the course back.

They stopped where the grass met the sandy beach area. Chris looked out over the water. While the sun wasn't quite setting yet, it was obvious it was going to be beautiful when it did. The rest of his view was pure water and sky, with peripheral trees and stones framing the cove at which the resort sat. Due to the fact that this lake was both deeper and farther north than the other great lakes, the water was rarely warm enough for most swimmers. There were always a few, though, brave enough to try it o ut.

The breeze coming straight down from Canada was warmed by the sun, both of which felt amazing on Chris' face. As he sat down in one of the chairs provided, he invited Boss Man to sit on his lap. "Can you see that ship in the distance?" he asked, pretty sure Boss' eyesight wasn't up to the challenge. "I wonder if you can smell it? Your nose seems pretty good."

Soon, the two of them were snoring in tandem, adjusting from time to time to ease the kinks in their muscles.

"Can I pet your dog?" Chris heard someone ask. Being half asleep, he ignored it. "Hey, Mister, can I pet your dog?" the kid repeated.

Boss Man moved, snapping Chris out of his much-needed nap. Suddenly realizing he was the "Mister" with the dog, he sat up to take stock of the situation. "Sure, he'd like that."

The young girl looked to be about ten years old. Her younger sister, maybe eight, wasn't as sure of the whole dog thing, but tagged along as younger siblings often do. Their dad was further back, making sure everyone behaved. Chris decided to make friends. "This is Boss Man. We sometimes call him 'Boss' for short."

The younger girl giggled, trying to hide it behind her hand.

"I'm Alyssa," said the older one, "and this is my sister Allie. She's pretty quiet. I usually do the talking." She carefully patted Boss on the head.

Boss Man, being quite fond of young humans, gave her his crooked-faced, missing-teeth smile. As she held her hand out to him, he added a few licks to her hand to show he approved. His slobber could not be contained, and the girl pulled her hand back with a grimaced face.

Chris laughed. "Slobber is how he tells you he loves you."

Not to be left out of all the attention, Allie squeaked out a softly spoken, "Can I pet him, too?"

"Absolutely, but only if you like dog slobber. "Chris said.

Allie grinned and carefully inched toward Boss, determined to conquer her fear. As her hand jerked forward and back in response to her internal war, the dog strained himself to sniff her scent. Clearly trying to encourage her, he licked the air in the direction of her hand. The accompanying shaking of his tail included his whole butt, which made him lose his balance on Chris' lap. Thankfully, Chris' quick reflexes averted the crisis.

Finally, the young girl made her way to Boss's neck. "Good boy", she said as he reciprocated the sentiment with a few licks. Allie was not nearly as averse to the reward as was her sister, but she did shriek with surprised excitement at the feeling of his tongue slurping across her arm.

"That a bulldog?" their father asked, nodding as he approached.

"English", answered Chris. "I just inherited him a couple of weeks ago. So far, we get along pretty well. He's friendly, despite his tough guy looks."

The man's face dropped. "My name's Carl. I'm so sorry for your loss."

"That's very kind of you. I'm Chris." As they shook hands, Chris explained further. "My uncle was sick for a long time, and the dog never left his side. He's grieved more than I have, as my uncle lived in Montana and I didn't really know him. I don't know that I could promise a dog many years, but since he's already 11, I figured I could give him back the loyalty he gave a sick old man. And, he's been decent company for me. I figured I'd bring him up here to see if I could get him out of his funk. So far, it seems to be working, but I'm not sure if it's the lakeshore or your daughters that has him so energetic." At this point, the girls were trying to pet Boss Man without letting him lick them. Boss was winning this game, and his snorts added to the shrieks of glee and bursts of giggles.

"Are you staying for the week?" Chris asked.

"Yeah. We came up from La Crosse. I work for the university there. You?"

"From Marshfield. ER nurse. I was only able to get a three-day weekend."

"I'll bet you've got some stories," said Carl.

Chris chuckled, "I'll bet you do, too."

"That I do." He then gestured toward the empty chair facing the lake next to Chris. With Chris' nod of approval, Carl eased himself into the chair. "I'm trying to give my wife a bit of a break so she can read in peace." He nodded toward a woman, clearly the mother of the two girls, who looked quite content to be slumped into a chair with a big novel on her lap.

The girls, having attached themselves to Boss Man, were engrossed in seeing the tricks he might know. Keeping a close eye on the trio, Carl and Chris swapped tales of life in their respective worlds.

"Dad, can I go get something from the cabin?" Alyssa asked.

"What do you want to get?"

"Um, I want to get something for Boss Man."

Carl looked at Chris. "Is he allowed to have people food? We've got some hot dogs. If it's ok, the girls could break one up for him."

"I think he would love that." Turning to Alyssa, Chris added, "But only one please, and break it up into small pieces. His teeth aren't that great anymore." Alyssa's face lit up as she skipped off to the family's cabin.

Boss Man was now laying belly side up next to Allie, who had long forgotten any fear she had of him. She was sitting with her legs stretched out before her, carefully petting his belly. "Boss Maaan, Boss Man, yooooou're the Boss Man," she sang, making it up as she went. A more adoring fan she could not have.

Upon Alyssa's return, the girls fed the gentle and grateful Boss Man his hot dog, nearly obsessing over making sure the pieces were small enough for him. Alyssa did not only bring treats, though. She also brought a pink tutu that quickly became the fashion statement of the day for their new four-legged friend. Both Chris and Carl felt a picture was required.

"I'm sorry to interrupt, but it's getting a little late and we talked about going out for dinner tonight," his wife said to Carl. Turning to Chris, she smiled and added, "Your dog is adorable. I'm Beth, by the way."

"Chris. Nice to meet you. Your girls have been giving the old Boss Man some very needed attention while Carl and I exchanged work stories." He looked at his watch. "Oh, wow, time flies, I guess! Yeah, Boss and I need to get going as well. We just got here this afternoon, so I need to get settled in for the night." Chris got up and took Boss Man's leash. "It was nice talking to you all. Hopefully we'll see you around the next day or two."

"Yeah, that sounds great," Carl and Beth replied in unison. The girls balked at first, but when promised they could play with the dog the next day, they begrudgingly took off his tutu and let him go.

Back in the cabin, Chris and Boss shared a little dinner and settled onto the sofa to watch some television. The air was perfect for sleeping under a pile of quilts until you couldn't sleep any more. Before long, another round of semi-synchronized snoring began.

Without warning, Boss Man shook himself awake and stood on the bed, sniffing the air. He sneezed out those smells and tried again. Clearly agitated, he spun in circles, waking up Chris.

"Boss, what is it? Do you need to go outside?"

Boss barked, jumping down from the bed and running to the door of the cabin. Chris followed, unlocking the door. Boss didn't wait. As soon as there was a narrow opening, he shoved himself out the door at full speed. Chris grabbed a jacket to put over his pajamas and slid on his shoes. He grabbed a flashlight as he fumbled out the door. "Where is he?" Chris asked, shining the flashlight to search for him. The barking helped him narrow it down.

Boss continued barking, having come to the door of one of the larger cabins. He demanded to be let in. "Boss Man, get back here!" Chris demanded as he continued to close the gap between them.

The door opened, and without so much as a recognition of the man who opened it, the dog shoved his way into the living room. "Boss Man?" Carl asked in disbelief. Boss ignored him, instead focusing on the smell. Left and left again, he ran into the girls' room and jumped on Allie's bed. He whimpered and laid next to her.

Carl ran after him, stopping short when he saw the dog just lying next to his daughter. The dog was not a threat to the girl, something was wrong. Chris followed suit, as the front door still open. "I have no idea what is happening," he stated flatly. "I am so sorry. He's never done this."

Beth came out of their bedroom wrapped in a robe to join the men at the door to their daughter's room. Alyssa, frozen behind a pillow in the other twin bed in the room, was struggling to wake up, her eyes blinded by the overhead light now on.

"Boss?" Chris asked, his mind racing to remember what he knew of his uncle, and trying to piece together what this all could mean.

Boss refused to move.

Chris stared at the young girl. The pieces came together quickly, but he had to be sure. "Is your daughter epileptic?" he asked.

"What?" Carl responded, his face contorted in shock and confusion.

"No, but I have an aunt that is," said Beth.

"I don't know if that's what is about to happen, but my uncle was a researcher on seizures."

The dog moved as Chris went to examine Allie.

Just then, Kristofer, the resort owner, came to the entrance of the cabin. "Is everything ok? Do you need some help?"

Chris identified himself as a nurse and instructed Kristofer to get the medical kit from his truck. "And call an ambulance", he added.

Turning to Carl and Beth, he reassured them. "She's breathing ok for now, but we need to make sure we know what we're dealing with. I don't know what Boss Man might be trained to detect." Allie's arms started to shake, causing Beth to gasp.

Carl instinctively went to pick her up, but Chris stopped him. "You can't pick her up. She's safer how she is, which is why the dog was trained to just lay by her. You can sit next to her and gently hold her head, though."

Alyssa started to cry, and Beth directed her instincts toward her older daughter. "She'll be ok, Honey," she said, rocking her gently.

Kristofer quickly returned with the medical kit in one hand, his phone in the other. The 911 dispatcher was already on the phone when he handed it to Chris. As Chris gave detailed medical information to the dispatcher, he occasionally asked the parents questions of family and medical history. The ambulance soon came, waking up any and all in the resort who were not already awake from the preceding commotion. They left swiftly, taking Allie and Beth with them.

Chris followed the ambulance closely, having refused to let Carl drive. Instead, Carl sat in the back seat of Chris' truck with Alyssa, telling her what he hoped to be true - that Allie would just need some medicine and would be fine. Honestly, though, he had never been so afraid in his life.

Chris asked the backseat passengers to be on alert for deer near the road. He knew from experience that giving people something to focus on gives them a sense of control in an out-of-control situation. They both vigilantly obeyed, scanning the roads and ditches as they moved through the darkness toward Marquette.

About five minutes in, Carl realized the bigger picture of what had happened. "What are the odds that a seizure sniffing dog and an ER nurse would be here tonight?"

"Pretty slim," answered Chris, "but this is definitely a story I'd have shared with you sitting by the water if it had happened before today".

"Yeah," answered Carl, still trying to wrap his head around everything happening. "But if you weren't there, what would have happened?"

"It's best not to speculate at this point. If it is epilepsy, there is a lot modern medicine can do for her. She's in good hands."

"Would...would you stay with us until we know?"

"Absolutely."

"Thank you. And thank you, Boss Man! You were a very, very good boy!" Boss Man, riding shotgun, grinned in the way old bulldogs do when they are proud.

"Good boy, Boss," Alyssa agreed. "How did he know, Dad?"

"That's a very good question."

Chris answered what he knew about his uncle's work. Nearly a decade before, the university his uncle worked for had conducted a series of studies on the ability of different breeds of dogs to be trained in predicting seizures and low blood sugar. While training to be a nurse, Chris remembered reading the studies. He was interested in the subject matter, but also in the family connection to the research. He did not, however, remember bulldogs being a part of those studies.

The night came and went, with Boss Man in the truck and Chris with the family in the hospital room. All seemed stable, and Chris needed a break, so he decided to check on Boss Man. While at the truck, he called his dad to see what he knew.

"Boss wasn't in those studies," his dad explained. "He was your Uncle Ken's pet. He took the dog to work with him. That dog helped him get through his divorce. They even retired together. I guess the dog just picked up on what was happening." His dad paused, then chuckled. "Your uncle would be beside himself to know how that dog reacted in the situation. Maybe they should have been studying bulldogs, hey?"

"Maybe," Chris agreed. "Thanks, dad, for the info."

"Hey, for what it's worth..."

"Yeah?"

"Those trained dogs are very expensive and hard to come by. You took Boss because you're a good person who wanted to make sure he was cared for. If you think he would be happy, and if he can help keep that girl safe... it wouldn't be a bad place for him to end up. The rest of the family would be ok with that. You know what I'm saying?"

"I do. This dog just grows on you though, you know?"

"I'm not saying you should hand him over, just that it wouldn't be wrong if that's what ended up happening, that's all."

"Understood. Thanks again, Dad."

"Anytime. But I want a picture of him in that tutu."

"I'll send it as soon as I hang up."

Chris leaned forward, putting his head in his hands. "You deserve to be retired," he mumbled, looking over at the passenger seat.

Within the blankets, a crumpled, snoring snout was all he could see of the now tired hero.

Chris pulled up the picture of the tutu-wearing dog and the girls on the beach and forwarded it as promised. Looking closer at the picture, he saw the crooked smirk on Boss Man's face. He was the happiest Chris had seen him since meeting him just two weeks ago. Many thoughts raced through his mind as he went back to the hospital room where the family waited for the rest of the answers.

"Where's Boss Man?" Allie asked, still groggy from being sleep deprived.

"He's under a blanket, all cozied up in my truck." Chris reassured her.

"He helped me. I was really scared," she said.

"Yeah, he was a really good boy," Chris agreed.

"Can he come sit by me?"

"I don't think they'll let him in here. He might slobber all over and make the doctors laugh too hard, and then they won't be able to do their job."

Allie smiled at the thought. "But isn't he the boss?"

"The doctor just has to release you, and then we can go home," said Carl.

"But can we go back to the cabin? I want to see Boss Man." Allie was now ready to cry.

Carl looked at Beth for back up. She shrugged her shoulders and said, "Well, the specialist at home can't see you until later in the week, and you should be ok until then. Maybe if we can get out of here today, you can visit with him until Chris takes him home."

Allie looked longingly at Chris.

"We can work that out," said Chris with a smile. Allie cheered, rousing her exhausted sister from the light sleep she was getting on the loveseat in the room.

The next day, a very soft knock on the door prompted a much louder bark from Boss. Chris, whose hair was quite disheveled, answered the door in his pajamas. Outside the door was a winded Alyssa, her dad still catching up to her. "Can Boss Man come over and play? Allie wants to see him."

"Of course, just give me a minute to get dressed, and we'll be right over."

As Chris and Boss Man entered the family's cabin, Chris could see the relief in Allie's face, as well as Beth's. Carl, however, seemed stressed. "While the kids and dog are getting reacquainted, could I ask you a few questions?"

Chris nodded, and the two of them stepped outside.

Carl took a deep breath before speaking. "Look, Boss Man wasn't the only one that saved my little girl, and I am highly aware of that. I don't know how to thank you for what you and your dog did." His face suggested he was struggling to find the words that matched his sentiment.

"It is my literal job, both as a nurse and as a fellow human being, to do my best to help in such a situation. But the doctors and nurses and medics - the whole team that treated her - and will continue to treat her - are just as responsible for the outcome. In fact, your family's efforts to learn what you can and comply with what the doctors tell you will go further into helping her than anything I did."

"What Boss did to alert us and the fact that he knew to lay next to her – how do I find a dog trained like that? The girls feel safe with him there, and to be honest, so do Beth and I."

Chris relayed the conversation he'd had with his dad about Boss Man's background, and how the dog learned by being around other dogs as they were being trained. "Often, a well-trained dog helps train a new generation. This dog is older. He's arthritic, so can't jump down from a truck or a high bed, but after seeing him playing with your girls, it's obvious he's got some life left in him. How would you feel about letting him train a younger d og?"

Carl's jaw dropped. "You mean...?"

"Look, I'm an ER nurse. I've made arrangements for him while I work, but to be honest, I'm not an ideal dog owner. I work anywhere from 12-24 hours in a shift. I took him because no one else in my family could, and we couldn't stand for him to go to people we didn't know. If you and Beth feel you can take on an elderly dog, as well as the training of a younger dog while learning how to care for your daughter... I mean, it's a lot all at once for your family, but I've been thinking about it all night, and I want what's best for him."

"Beth and I spent a lot of the night talking about this. We can afford for her to be home with the girls, and having a dog - dare I say, two dogs, would be good company for them, and a comfort for the reality of our lives now. He saved our girl, and may continue to save her. He could not be a part of a more grateful family."

"Not going to lie," said Chris, "I'm going to miss him. He just grows on a guy."

Well, let's ask him, shall we?" Carl said. The men shook on the matter, and went back inside.

"Come on, Boss man, let's go!" Chris said, softly. Boss whined, plopping his butt on the floor. "The Boss has spoken, I guess."

Beth looked at Carl, wide-eyed at the possibility that someone would just give them the dog of their dreams. Carl grinned back. "I guess we're under new management," he said with a laugh.

"If you give me your contact info, I can email you his vet records and everything I know about him. Make sure you don't give him cheese, though. His farts will clear a room if you do!"

As Chris packed his belongings into his truck, he couldn't help but feel like he'd been a part of something pretty amazing. The family promised to send pictures and to keep him included in how things progressed. How odd, he thought, that he came up here to help the dog get over his past, but instead gave him a future. Chris knew he would miss him, but he also knew Boss Man needed that family as much as they needed him.

He decided to add his name to the guestbook before leaving.

Name: Chris V.
From: Marshfield
Highlight: One very, very good dog.

Hearing Myself Whisper

"**I** just need . . . hang on."

Standing on the porch of the cabin, Evie struggled to keep her phone out of the sideways rain while trying to read the passcode she was sent.

"Are you still there?" The voice on the other end yelled, trying to be heard through the storm.

"Let me call you back."

"But...."

She hung up, exasperated with the conversation, her situation and the increasingly cold rain. A flash of lightning blinded her for a split second. She jumped, but then her eyes finally caught the number.

"1, 7, 3, 6, open!" Nearly falling into the cabin, she caught herself on the doorframe. The contents of her purse spilled into the room, adding to her frustration. *Why does this have to be so hard?*

Hanging up her jacket near the door, Evie caught a glimpse of herself in the mirror. Dark streaks of mascara slid down her face, causing her to wonder if it was the rain or her tears of frustration causing the issue. The frown she saw bothered her more, but she couldn't think about that now. She kicked off her shoes and headed to the bathroom for a towel.

The sound of the ringtone from her purse on the table felt like a weight that settled into her shoulders and neck. His insecurity was controlling them both, and she needed to figure out how to stop that influence. At the moment, though, she resolved herself to be understanding. After all, this wasn't his normal way of dealing with her. Her answer must have thrown him for quite a loop. With a deep breath, she answered his call. "Hello Hon. I'm sorry for the delay in calling you back, I was getting settled in. The storm must be coming off of the lake. I'm completely drenched."

"Can I drive up there and take you out for lunch tomorrow?"

Her annoyance was hard to hide. "That would defeat the purpose of my being here."

"But we can talk about this," he begged.

"I have a lot of changes happening in my life very quickly, and I just need some time to get my head wrapped around them. If you can't give me a couple of days to figure things out, then..."

"But I don't understand. I thought this was what you wanted – what we both wanted?"

"Look, I love being with you. When we're together, though, I work on figuring out how you feel, and how to make you happy."

"I know, and I love that about you, Evie. You care so much about others."

"But I need to know myself — how I feel, and what will make me happy. I have to do that in solitude. I know this is hard to understand, but for me, other people's emotions seem to yell, and mine only whisper."

The silence made her wonder if the call dropped.

"Am I that overbearing?" came his eventual reply.

"Please — this is not about you, or whether you would be a great husband! It's just how I work. Please trust me that I am not running away from you. You have made me an amazing offer, and I am sure you would make an excellent husband."

"I feel a 'but' coming here," he replied.

"But I literally got my master's degree a week ago. This is a lot. I can't tell you my answer right now, but I can tell you that if I don't have the time I need to think - without anyone here - I most definitely cannot give you a 'yes'."

Defeated, he acquiesced. "Ok. Will you call me if you decide before you come back?"

"I think it would be cruel to not give you an answer as soon as I have one."

"There you go again, being thoughtful even when I am not. I'm sorry for trying to rush you. It's just that I guess I thought we were both ready."

"And I might be, it's just that I need to sort it out. Thank you for understanding. I do really love you, and I will see you in a couple of days."

"I love you too, Evie."

The disappointment in his voice was crushing, but she stood her ground. They said their good nights and she hung up, grateful that he had not added the pressure of making his proposal public. The last thing she needed was to have well-meaning friends and family getting their opinions involved.

She started the fireplace and pulled out the bottle of wine she picked up on the way. A glass of wine and the large club chair in front of the fire was the perfect setting to mull over the options life was offering.

A good night's sleep was followed by a disappointing realization. *How could you forget the coffee?* she asked herself incredulously. Shuffling to the kitchen, she found a couple of single serve options, but neither of them seemed worthy of self-care. Determined to settle for nothing short of a perfect weekend on her own, she was soon dressed and eager to find a coffee shop with something made just for her.

Before climbing into her car, she turned to take in the view she missed on arrival. The sky held remnants of last night's storm, progressing from dark grey to pillowy white fluff to a peaceful patch of blue. Still wet from the rain, the trees below were a patchwork of green with orange and yellow accents. The white cabins dotted the park-like grounds. Her cabin stood out as the only log one, a steadfast piece of history among the tides of progress. She drew a slow deep breath of the cool moist air, wanting to savor every moment of her time here.

Suddenly aware of the tension in her shoulders, she stretched to release the strain.

"Hello! Where are you from?"

The older woman coming toward her seemed to want to catch her before she got in the car, but her version of hurrying required Evie to wait for her. Badly needing either a new hip or knee, the woman's face showed no sign of the pain her gait betrayed. Instead, she beamed with the delight of a stranger about to become a friend.

"Ah, Green Bay. You?"

"Chicago," the woman said. As they shook hands, the woman continued. "My name is Phyllis. I was raised here, but my family is all gone now. This one back over there is my husband, Dave." As she pointed behind her, Dave nodded in the background almost on cue. "He's the reason I'm now from Chicago. Four kids and six grandkids later, and here we are."

"I'm Evelyn, but my friends call me Evie. It's nice to meet you, Phyllis.

"You here with someone, Evie?"

"I'm only here until Monday morning." Evie looked down at the car keys in her hands, fidgeting with them as she spoke. "I, ah-I came to get some time to myself."

"Well, I don't mean to take that away from you, but if you feel you'd like a little break in the seclusion, Dave and I are having a nice fire tonight, and we'd love to have you. We love meeting new people. I even brought some of my homemade apple pie. It tastes even better warmed up over the fire."

Much to Evie's surprise, the words "That sounds wonderful! What time?" escaped her mouth before she thought about it. Since no damage was done, she decided to just go with it and enjoy the company.

Putting a hand over her eyes to protect them from the bright sun, Phyllis laid out the details. "We usually wait until the sun is almost down, but not quite. That way there's enough light to start the fire, but enough darkness to really enjoy it. We're done by midnight, though. Nothing good happens after midnight, as they say."

"I'll be there. I'm doing a little exploring today, but should be back well before dark. What can I contribute?"

Phyllis whispered from the back of her hand, as if her husband could hear them from two cabins over. "Dave always brings so much food, we don't have to go to the store for a solid two weeks after we get home. I have no idea what makes him think we won't have enough. There's only two of us, can you imagine?!?"

Evie looked past Phyllis' shoulder to see Dave dragging a large, wheeled cooler with a second one on top of it. The situation looked sketchy, and before she could decide whether to say something, the small cooler slid off the big one, landing perfectly upright as if Dave planned it that way. The way he hunched his shoulders and froze when he heard the thud of the cooler landing on the ground, however, proved this was not the case.

Evie looked back at Phyllis in time to be on the receiving end of a knowing wink. She could not help but be amused.

Later, Evie found her way to the Falling Rock Cafe, where she ordered a breakfast sandwich and a cappuccino from the cheerful woman behind the counter. A small table near the large front window gave her the view of those coming and going through downtown Munising. As she bit into the warm sandwich, Evie thought about how refreshing a vacation alone was, even if unplanned. Everything seemed better here. The air seemed clearer, the food tastier — *thinking of you, breakfast sandwich* — and the smell of the lake was unique. She couldn't place the difference between the smell of Lake Superior versus Lake Michigan, but she knew they were different. Not better or worse, just both their own kind of good. There was a freedom here — a freedom of knowing no one and owing no explanation for herself or her feelings. *I should do this more often,* she thought. She then wondered if just being on vacation made everything better. Would she really need to be alone to enjoy it, or would she find happiness in sharing it with Matt?

A bicycle whizzed by the window, catching her off guard. The cappuccino nearly spilled down the front of her shirt. It took a moment for her to realize it had not, and instead left only a small splash on the table. Using her napkin to wipe the spill, she reprimanded herself for letting her mind wander. This wasn't a vacation, this was a working weekend. A major life decision needed to be made.

Checking her purse for the tools needed to do the job, Evie found her standard requirements. With a wire binding at the top and a line down the middle of the page, her steno book was the perfectly neutral notebook for any major life decision. On the left she wrote, "Pros", and on the right she wrote "Cons", as she had done so many times before.

"He makes me laugh," she muttered under her breath as she wrote. This was of utmost importance, as she took herself way too seriously. Her serious side liked to make mountains out of molehills, and his ability to shrink them back down to manageable size was important. The cons were harder to articulate. She struggled to write them, fearing that somehow acknowledging them this way would make them more real.

"And he's balanced. Yes, definitely a pro, not a con." Evie added it to her list.

An hour flew by as her list grew, the cons starting to take shape, though the list was short. Finally, she could think of no more pros and no more cons. Her brain was tired of emotional thinking, and it needed a break. Shoving the offending notebook and pen back into her purse for later, Evie ordered another cappuccino, this time to go. She checked the lid to make sure it was tight before browsing through the books in the café. After careful scrutiny, she purchased two books, one on the history of Munising, and one on Lake Superior shipwrecks. Each would be a lovey addition to her growing history-based collection, and ones she was eager to read.

Not satisfied with just reading on her trip, Evie decided to get all she could out of her time here. She would think about Matt later, for now, she just wanted to live a little. That feeling caught her off guard, and she felt a pang of guilt over thinking of Matt as someone she needed freedom from. Was it just the idea of marriage, or him personally?

A sign for a cruise along the lakeshore called out to her sense of adventure, and she soon found herself aboard. Enamored with the rugged coastline, she had to force herself to put her phone camera down from time to time and enjoy the scenery in real life.

By the time she had hiked a waterfall and had taken a selfie, she was feeling more alone and less at ease with the idea that she'd not made a decision.

After a little shopping, she stopped for dinner and reread her list. Something was missing from the list, but she couldn't figure out what it was. She tried starting over on a fresh piece of paper, but no new information came to light.

At the end of the day, still uneasy with the layers yet to uncover, Evie pulled into the parking area near her cabin. "I'll be right over," she said, waving to Phyllis. "I just have to bring some stuff inside first".

"No hurry, we'll be here," said Phyllis.

In the background, Dave was using a blow torch and old newspaper to start the fire.

That's a guy who doesn't like to do things halfway, Evie thought. *Ok, bathroom break and then fill the water bottle, and that should be everything.* She punched in the code, dropped her findings on the table, and got ready to meet her entertainment for the evening.

As Evie walked over to their cabin, she thought about how she would explain Matt. Boyfriend? Fiancé? She couldn't think of a reason to say no to his proposal, so she was beginning to think it was just nerves. Still, she wasn't quite ready to call him fiancé, it just felt odd. *Boyfriend, it is.*

In her walk over, she watched Dave unfold a third chair they'd brought for guests. Apparently, they even knew to plan for new friends. "Hello! The fire looks great. Thanks for having me."

Dave nodded and gestured for her to have a seat.

"Glad you can make it," greeted Phyllis, getting up from her chair. "I'll go get the pie. Dave, can you make sure she has something to drink?" Phyllis was already halfway in the cabin by the time she finished asking.

"Oh, I brought my water bottle, but thank you."

"Well, when that runs dry, we have hot chocolate, tea, and the makings for a brandy old-fashioned," Dave replied. "Phyllis has one a week."

"If you make them every week for her, you must be good at it."

"I sure am. They go great with the apple pie. Where was it you said you were from?"

"Green Bay, born and raised."

"Ah, a true Cheesehead!" he teased.

Before Evie could answer, Phyllis burst out of the door of the cabin, cast iron skillet full of apple pie in her hand. "You betcha, Dave, she's on my side of things, and don't you be spreading your Bears' propaganda up here! We're not in Chicago today."

Evie laughed, sure that Dave knew just when to call her a cheese head to get the best reaction from Phyllis. She mused, too, at how quickly Phyllis' Yooper accent came back, though they'd lived so long in Chicago.

"How long have you two been married?" Evie asked.

Phyllis looked at Dave.

"Oh, is it my turn to do the math?" he said, "Let's see . . . 45 years this winter."

"Wow, that's wonderful! Clearly it couldn't have always been so easy. Any advice for someone who's not quite there yet?"

"Are you planning to be?"

"Dave, she may not want to talk about that." Phyllis half whispered.

Evie adjusted herself in the chair, suddenly self-conscious. "No. Well, actually . . . maybe it would be good if I did." Evie paused to gauge the reaction on their faces before proceeding.

"Is that why you're here, Honey?" Phyllis asked quietly.

"My boyfriend, Matt. He, uh, proposed to me yesterday. I haven't given him an answer yet, and I told him I needed some time to myself to think."

"Well, I don't see anything wrong in making sure," said Dave.

"I recently finished my master's degree and it just . . . feels like a lot at once." Evie stared into the fire, finally addressing the feelings she'd been running from all day. "I think it hurt his feelings that it wasn't an immediate decision, but I just couldn't spit out the word, 'Yes'." She looked from Dave to Phyllis. "I also couldn't say no. He's what every girl wants. He's handsome, he's kind, he has a measure of financial security, and I do love him. Seems a no-brainer, right?"

"Well, sure, if you like that sort of thing," Dave quipped, winking at Phyllis.

Sliding the skillet onto the grate over the fire, Phyllis pointed out the obvious. "A decision this big should never be a no-brainer. He sounds great on paper, but that's not how we choose someone to spend our lives with. We need both the mind and the heart. What specifically attracts you to him?"

"Well, he is very kind, even when things go wrong and he is dealing with a rude person. He wants me to help him in the family business, which would be a very...nice life." She looked down at her feet. "So why don't I sound very excited? I can't figure out the problem that makes me not just want to jump on the chance to accept."

The silence held for a moment while they all processed her words.

"What do your parents think?" Phyllis asked as she moved the skillet, warming the whole pie. The smell of apples and cinnamon mingled with wood smoke wafted up, offering a preview of the homemade goodness to come.

"I haven't asked them. I didn't want to be influenced one way or another. I figured since neither of you know him, and you barely know me, I wasn't quite as worried about telling you."

Dave wriggled in his chair, uncomfortable in his observation. "What's your degree in?"

"World history, with a minor in literature."

"Ooh, the girl with the big stories!" Dave chided eagerly with an approving nod. "And what kind of business is Mr. Matt's family in, if you don't mind my asking?"

"His family runs a string of hotels in Northeastern Wisconsin. It's based in Green Bay."

"Well, I don't know if this is what's got you scared, but if you were my daughter, I'd tell you to think twice."

"Now Dave, that's a pretty quick answer to an awfully big decision. This might be the right guy for her, how do you know?" Phyllis retorted.

"I'll tell you what, you put a piece of that pie on a plate for me, and I'll explain while I make you an old-fashioned." Phyllis smiled as she grabbed a knife and a spatula to get to work while Dave turned to Evie. "Would you like an old-fashioned yourself, young lady?"

"I think maybe I will," she replied.

Dave stepped over to the makeshift bar he set up before building the fire and started muddling the sugar, bitters, and water, which he had so entertainingly splashed into the three cups set up for just such a purpose. "Don't get me wrong now, he doesn't sound like a bad guy. In fact, he seems pretty nice."

"He is," Evie agreed, happy to defend him.

"So then, what would you do with your degree if you helped run the hotel business?"

Evie laughed nervously. "I'm not sure. I guess I just hadn't really thought about it." That was it! That was what was missing from her list. *Why hadn't I thought about it? This is a big deal, right? Or was it?*

While she contemplated this, Phyllis handed Evie the most heavenly scented apple pie she had ever smelled.

"This looks amazing!"

"Ope! Forgot the ice cream. Dave, can you put a quick scoop on there for our girl here?"

Dave handed Evie the expertly crafted brandy old-fashioned first, then ducked into the cabin, leaving her to contemplate his question. She blew on the steamy apples to cool it off a little before trying it. While her first forkful was on its way to her taste buds, Dave dropped a scoop of vanilla bean on the plate next to it. The pie and ice cream immediately started melding together.

Evie savored her first bite while dreading the answer to what she was about to say. "A lot of people don't end up in the fields they went to school for."

"How I see it," Dave explained while dishing out scoops for Phyllis and himself, "nearly any smart person could help him run his hotel business. Nothing wrong with that. But he's not dating just any smart person. He's dating someone who has spent her life working on learning the history of our world and how to teach it to others through writing, am I right?"

"Well, yeah, I guess."

"So, he wants you to set all that aside in order to be part of a family-run business where, if you ever split up, your hard work goes toward his profits and you walk away owning nothing."

"Well, that could be worked out in a prenup, if need be, but I don't like the idea of planning for divorce."

"You know," Phyllis added, "Dave and I met in college. I wanted to be a teacher, but back in our day, once the kids came, the wife automatically stayed home."

"And she was a teacher. First at home with our kids, but then she eventually got a job at the school, and used her gifts to help more than just our family. We have so many cards and letters from students she taught over the years, and the difference she made in their lives. Can you imagine her selling cars with me? What a waste that would have been." He paused for a moment, looking up at the moon. "I'm not saying he's a bad man, or that he doesn't love you, but where does all your schooling fit into his business plans?"

"I'll need to think about that," Evie replied, "But that does seem to be the aspect I'd been missing." Tears welled up in her eyes as relief and guilt mingled. How could she not have seen this herself?

"Oh, Honey, we didn't mean to hurt your feelings," Phyllis exclaimed while handing her a napkin.

"You didn't! Actually, I can't explain why, but I feel so relieved. I also feel horrible that I couldn't put this into words before."

Phyllis moved her chair next to Evie's and placed her hand on Evie's shoulder. "None of us knows everything about ourselves. Sometimes we have to go through things to find out who we are and what we want. Plus, maybe you didn't feel this way until you were staring down the barrel of forever in the role."

Evie turned to her and smiled. "This weekend is the first time I have felt like who I am has value without being attached to someone else since... In fact..." She trailed off, a flood of memories rushing in on her. Suddenly, she could see more cons; many more cons, especially as she thought of a future in the hospitality industry. She always saw herself working at a museum or a national park. She needed to call Matt, and she needed to do it immediately. "I need to make a phone call, I..."

Evie sobbed herself to sleep that night. Neither the fireplace nor the waves gently lapping on the shore could soften the blow of having to break the heart of a man she held so dear. It was hard to tell, though, if her pain was compassion for him, or for herself. She narrowly escaped a situation that would have made her toss aside her life's passions, to be replaced with a life that would make her a resentful and bitter woman. How could she have been so blind for so long?

In the long day since the proposal, Matt had increasingly come to expect a refusal, and by the time it came, he begrudgingly accepted it. Being a truly good-intentioned man, he came to understand what he was really asking her to become, and he knew it wasn't right. Matt knew she would come to resent him, and he'd rather be loved as a friend than to be resented as a husband.

With all the crying and emotional exhaustion from the night before, Evie drank a bottle of water as quickly as she reasonably could, trying to rehydrate herself and ease the accompanying headache.

The smell of bug spray and smoke, mixed with the feel of dried tears and unbrushed teeth made a shower her first priority. As the warm water hit her face and scalp, she began to feel human again. The muscles in her back loosened, and her arms fell to her side as she waited for the conditioner to do its work. Her mind couldn't spin anymore on her decision. Her conversation with Matt, though difficult, confirmed she'd made the right choice. The only thing left for her to do was decompress. After that, she would tell her friends and family they were through.

The phone rang, much to her dismay. Probably a friend who'd heard already. She ignored it, not having the emotional stamina to explain everything. She chose, instead, to go sit by the lake. She still had the cabin until tomorrow, and she was not going to waste it. This was going to be a weekend of self-discovery.

A row of Adirondack chairs grouped in twos dotted the grass that led to the beach. She brought her big blanket and her bottle of water and curled up. She watched the waves glisten in the sunlight as her lungs worked to sync to the rhythmic sounds they made.

"Good morning!"

"Good morning, Phyllis," she said as her new friend sat down.

"Do you mind if I sit with you for a few minutes?" With a nod from Evie, she sat. "I guess I should have asked before I sat down, because these chairs are not that easy to get out of. Looks like I may need Dave to help me get out. Quite a predicament indeed," she lamented, looking around to see what she could use as a tool to help her stand up.

"I'm actually glad you're here," Evie said.

"This is one of those time where it feels like something has been ripped out of you, but that's where the new good things grow," said Phyllis.

They talked for nearly an hour about children, grandchildren, and teaching. Evie loved every minute of it, and the conversation seemed to make her even more motivated to do with her life the things she dreamed about, just as Phyllis had done. "It's not that I haven't made my sacrifices," Phyllis pointed out, "but when it's the right person and both sides are making sacrifices, it doesn't feel like you're really sacrificing anything. Dave used to make dinner twice a week so I could take refresher classes before going into a teaching job."

"What if there is no right person?"

"What do you mean?"

"Do I have to *have* someone to *be* someone? I mean, I don't want to disparage marriage. I'd like to be married someday . . . maybe. But I was ready to make a commitment that would likely have made me a very bitter woman in time."

"What are you thinking you want to do then?"

"That's what I am trying to figure out. I'm due to go home in the morning, but maybe I need a little more time to make a life plan. There has to be more than just a career out there for me."

Phyllis leaned back in her chair and thought over what that meant.

Evie explained further. "You know, there are many ways for a person to be loved. The love of friends and family aren't nearly appreciated enough in our culture. Romantic love, on the other hand, is so glorified that many a poor decision has been made in the pursuit of it. Yes, it's a wonderful thing, but there are many wonderful things in life that we can be blessed to enjoy."

"Exactly," said a voice coming up behind them. Dave, quite stealthy up to that point, had come to remind Phyllis of their appointment for lunch.

"You'll have to help me out of this chair first," she teased, leaning forward and putting out her hand.

Dave pulled her up, directly toward him where his other arm caught and stabilized her. The sweetness of the exchange tugged at Evie, who suddenly second-guessed everything she just said. *It would be nice to be married*, she thought. *Otherwise, who would help me out of a chair when I'm older?*

"Good thing I came along," Dave teased.

"My good friend Evie here would have helped me, I'm sure."

Evie smiled, realizing Phyllis just answered her question. "I absolutely would have," she answered.

Enjoying some popcorn and a cup of tea in front of the fireplace, Evie decided to stop mulling and start exploring. She opened her tablet and pulled up a career app. In the search bar, she typed, "History", the location field she left blank. For hours, she scrolled through career options newly opened to her. She compared salary ranges with costs of living, housing opportunities, and the culture of the area. No longer was she limited to a limited distance from anything. The thought both scared and excited her, as she bookmarked opportunities she'd like to apply for once she returned home.

In the morning, she made one last tour of the cabin to make sure she didn't forget anything. The guestbook caught her eye. Fascinated, she glanced down the list of names, cities, and comments about the highlights of those who came before her. Waterfalls and coffee shops, restaurants, fish, and even an occasional honeymoon were noted. What part would she play in the history of this cabin? □

Name: Evie
From: Green Bay
Highlight:

She paused, trying to decide whether to write about the people or the places. There were a lot of good things about this weekend, but one thing stood out as more significant than the rest. With a smile on her face, she put her pen to paper.

Highlight: Hearing myself whisper

The Elusive Kirtland's Warbler

An hour before sunrise, a robin perched on the roof of the cabin and joyfully sang the first notes of the dawn chorus. A nearby thrush joined in just after eating his breakfast.

Miles took no notice of their efforts, instead focusing on the contents of his daypack now strewn across the table before him. As he placed each item in the bag, he lifted his chin to see the checklist and drew a line through the entry, completely ignoring the checkboxes on the left.

Rebecca, who only came for the road trip and some peace and quiet, was amused at the intense focus he was expending for such a task. She hid her face behind a feigned sip of coffee and whispered, "Check," as he crossed off each item.

Unfazed by her humor, he zipped the daypack closed, patted it twice for good measure, and placed it near the door before finishing his coffee. Today was going to be his day, he just knew it.

As Miles put the last of his things in the car, a man three cars over popped open the hatch to his vehicle and started digging.

"Good morning," the man greeted, holding up his binoculars. As he spoke, a lens cap fell off and rolled down the parking lot.

"Morning, Bill," replied Miles, amused by the sight of his brother running after the cap. "Ready to see some birds?"

"Looking forward to it!" Bill grabbed his lens cap and put his things in the back seat of Miles' car. He then climbed into the passenger seat and asked, "So what do I need to know?"

"It's mostly just trying to make them comfortable enough to want to be around us. The hard part of being new is trying to remember the names of the birds you're seeing. Just go out and look at them and try to match them to the app."

"Ok, sounds good. I did get that downloaded."

"Great! That'll help a lot." The sun's rays came over the horizon directly in front of them. Miles felt it in the back of his eyes. "Woah, that's bright," he murmured, lowering the visor. It didn't help much, but his eyes were adjusting.

As they headed toward their destination, Miles wondered if his brother would ever be ready to retire. It seemed the life of a paramedic was a constant adrenaline rush. Could Bill learn to slow his pace and enjoy a more peaceful way of life? Miles frowned, thinking of how Bill's stressful job and subsequent divorce took their toll on his health. He shook his head, trying to erase his concerns. After all, this weekend was to be a foregleam of their time together in retirement. Bill was just six months from his last day at work, and already was looking to buy a house in their hometown. Miles was eager for them to spend a lot more time together.

"So, what is this bird you're wanting to see?" Bill asked, pulling up the app on his phone.

Miles was happy for the change of focus. "It's called the 'Kirtland's Warbler".

"Kirtland's Warbler? Never heard of it." He typed the name into the app to see the pictures.

"It's a small grey bird with a yellow belly. Probably one of the rarest songbirds in North America. It likes the young Jack Pines here. If I see one, I'll show you."

In the year since his retirement, Miles had been adding to his journal each species as he identified them. The more common ones helped him learn basic identification, but the more rare birds, like the Kirtland's Warbler, were what would take him to the next level as a birder. He'd researched the more likely spots, determined to find one. This weekend, he set his sights on the Anderson Lake Parkway, hoping the Kirtland's Warblers shared his instinct.

"The bugs don't seem too bad," Bill said as he slung his bag chair over his shoulder. He grabbed his daypack and closed the car door.

"We have the wind working for us today, otherwise the black flies would be awful this time of year. Here's some bug spray, just in case the breeze dies down".

Walking toward their destination, Miles stopped short. "See that one over there, the one upside down?" He asked, pointing to the side of a tree just ahead.

"Yeah, I think I see the one you're talking about," Bill said, putting his binoculars up to his face.

"That's a nuthatch."

"How do you know it's a nuthatch?" he asked as it flew away.

"Mostly because they like to be upside down." Miles continued on, with Bill right behind him. "If you look on your app once we get settled, you'll see there are a number of different ways to identify a bird."

"Do you hear that?" Miles asked, looking toward the sound, but seeing only leaves.

"Which one?"

"The one that sounds like, 'Cheer-cheer-cheer'."

"Yeah, what is that?"

"It's a cardinal. They're common, but if you have some at your bird feeder, it's still pretty nice." Miles lifted his chin to look through his bifocals at Bill. "They're always cheerful." The small smirk on his face revealed the pun was intentional.

"Yeah, I know what a cardinal looks like, just didn't know they sounded like that. Cool!"

About half a mile later, Miles paused again. "That's our spot, right in there." He pointed to the small clearing on the left. The men climbed over downed trees and broken branches to make their way to the grassy area. "Watch to make sure we don't disturb any nests," Miles warned. "These things make their nests on the ground".

Bill stopped and looked at him, confused. "Why would they do that?"

"I don't judge," Miles answered, walking past him.

"I'm not judging them, I just want to know why they do what they do," he answered, walking again to catch up.

"Well, if we find one, we can ask them. Ah, here we go," Miles announced. The semi-shaded area near the edge of the clearing was ideal, with a few young Jack Pines dotting the area.

"It's getting quiet," Bill said as he placed his chair just out of reach of the branch of a large tree.

"The birds will sing again, we just have to be quiet and still." Miles smirked as he watched Bill unwittingly put his chair on an anthill, wondering how long it would take him to realize the error. Wanting to avoid being a part of what was to come, Miles set up his chair in the sun, about ten yards away, facing Bill.

Donning his sun hat and binoculars, he mentally transformed from Everyday Miles to Miles, Birder Extraordinaire. The small cutting board he used for a lap desk and his journal slid easily from his daypack. "Birder mode activated," he whispered to himself. He listened intently and began listing the birds he saw and heard as the morning resumed.

"AAAAAAAHH!" Nearly flying from his chair, Bill began what could only be described as a violent assault on the army of ants now crawling on his legs. "WHY?" He yelled, as if expecting the ants to explain themselves.

Miles' countenance remained stoic, but it took everything he had to keep it that way. "Looks like you sat on an anthill there."

"They're attacking me!" Bill yelled, swatting them off.

"Well, you sat on their house."

Bill stopped fighting the ants long enough to give a hostile stare. "Shut up!" he retorted.

Miles' stoic demeanor broke, and the lemonade he'd just taken a sip of spewed out of his mouth in laughter. He watched in amusement while Bill moved his chair to a spot that had neither birds above nor an anthill below.

In time, Bill stopped checking his legs for ants and began to relax. With his contentment came the return of the birds' melodious reminders that all was well.

As the morning continued, a slight on and off again buzzing sound joined the symphony. To Miles, the tune of this one seemed off, and as the volume and voracity increased, so did his annoyance. His ears located the sound, directing his eyes to the offender by turning his head slightly to the right.

Bill, draped awkwardly in the chair, was snoring.

Miles was torn, but only slightly. As much as he wanted to see the warbler, he could not allow the opportunity before him to be ignored. He hadn't forgotten how Bill enlisted Rebecca's help to replace every picture of him in their home with that of a circus clown. It took a week for him to notice, and even then, a dinner guest had to point it out. Looking back, he realized this had been one of his brother's best pranks.

Not to be outdone, Miles got up from his chair and grabbed a small bag of birdseed from his backpack. His footsteps were careful and methodical, his face determined, as he made his way over to Bill's chair. Opening the small bag of seed, he poured some in his hand. Taking one pinch at a time, he placed his hand just above the divot at the top of Bill's sun hat, making sure the seed was neither felt nor heard.

The snoring stopped. Miles froze, hoping to not be noticed. He held his breath, then slowly, nearly imperceptibly even to himself, he let it out. Bill groaned and rearranged, his eyes remaining closed. The small amount of birdseed fell from the divot of the hat to the brim, unnoticed by its wearer.

Miles continued still, allowing himself to focus on the birdsong again until the snoring resumed. Adding seed to the divot went decidedly quicker now, as Miles nervously balanced the thin line between not wanting to be discovered and running out of time.

The seed pile soon filled a third of the divot, enough to draw the birds. As quietly and methodically as he had come, he returned to his own chair and readied his phone camera.

Once the snoring stopped, it took exactly seven minutes for a black-capped chickadee to find the new buffet. The small and light bird landed, ate a couple of seeds and took off, unnoticed by the still slumbering Bill. Shortly afterwards, a small yellow and grey bird landed on the hat. Miles zoomed in his camera. Could it be? Could it actually be? He was unsure, but pressed the button.

The angry streak of blue and white from a blue jay filled the screen as the phone registered the shot. Miles' attention left the phone screen in time to see Bill flailing his arms like a madman. The mutual sounds of shock and disdain filled the clearing as the blue jay darted to the safety of the nearby tree branch.

Bill, now holding his hat in one hand and checking his head for blood drawn with another, stared at Miles. "What just attacked me?"

"According to the angry screeching from that tree over there, that would be a blue jay," Miles answered.

Bill turned toward the trees and yelled, "Well, I know what a blue jay looks like! Count your days, bird!"

"Did it draw blood?" He felt a little guilty that the bird had actually pecked Bill's head, which wasn't part of his plan. Bill, however, seemed like his ego was hurt more than anything.

Bill turned to Miles. "Stupid thing attacked me in my sleep! How is this even interesting to you? They just fly around and poop. See?" He held up his hat, revealing a large white splotch of evidence.

For a moment, Miles forgot all about identifying the warbler, instead focusing on the incredulous look on Bill's face. A smirk broke the deadpan veil, followed by a full smile and then a chuckle. Miles' self-control then completely caved, as a full belly laugh took over.

"It seems I scared him more than he scared me," Bill said, now laughing at the mess on his hat. "I'm going to need a bathroom. Where were they again?"

Without a word, Miles opened his backpack and handed Bill a zip-top bag containing a trowel, biodegradable toilet paper, and hand sanitizer.

"Oh...ok then," Bill said as he took the bag begrudgingly.

"Watch out for ants," Miles yelled as Bill made his way back toward the path.

Hours later, Bill was able to identify some of the more common birds in the area, and Miles had added two more to his list. The Kirtland's Warbler, however, was not one of them. The photo of what he hoped was the rare bird, instead was a blue and white wing on it's way from Bill's hat, with a part of Bill standing up from his chair behind it. Miles was unsure which picture would have been more rare, and decided he was happy with the story this one caught.

"I'm sorry, Miles, but I'm kind of done for the day. The bugs are just getting too hungry."

Miles nodded in agreement. Disappointed as he was, the biting flies were now fighting the breeze, and the bug spray was of little use. The men packed up their things and headed out.

Miles started to ask a question as he pulled out of the parking spot, but then stopped. "Do you hear that noise?"

"Yeah, what is that?"

"I don't know." Miles put the car in park and checked under the hood.

"Almost sounds like engine knock," said Bill. "Let me see what's near here for auto repair."

"I think we'd better have it checked out," Miles agreed.

"I heard you coming," said the cheerful woman at the counter as they walked in the door of Joe and Sons Auto Repair.

"We were in the area looking for birds, and my car started making that noise. I'm hoping someone can just tell me if it's drivable. If so, can I worry about it when I get back home, or would it need to be fixed immediately? We're only in town for the weekend."

"I'm pretty sure Aaron can squeeze in a quick peek before his next appointment. If it's quick and we have the parts, he might even be able to get to it this afternoon."

"Great, thanks," replied Miles, handing her the keys.

Bill picked up a magazine to read and sat down to wait. Miles sat near him, slightly unsettled at the thought of a large repair bill.

"Hopefully it's not the whole engine," Bill said, coming out of the restroom with a newly cleaned hat. "You never know about these things."

Miles was already doing the math in his head, the decision to fix or replace not obvious. Depending on how bad the bill was, this was a decision he did not want to make alone. Uneasy, he made the call to Rebecca. "Hey, Sweetheart, so...ah...Bill and I are at a car repair shop. It's making a noise that sounds like engine knock. Could be...hold on."

He watched as the mechanic came out and looked toward a woman standing behind the desk on her cell phone, clearly finishing up the details of a business transaction. When she hung up, he gestured her to follow him. With a quizzical look on her face, she followed Aaron back to the car.

"I'm going to have to call you back." Miles hung up the phone and watched through the doorway to the shop area as the mechanic pointed to the undercarriage of the car. He watched as the woman began to take pictures. *Oh, this is bad*, he thought as he watched her walk toward him.

She asked him to come into the shop to see it, then closed the door behind them. "Miles, right?" she asked.

"Yes."

"My name is Rylee. I'm the owner. This is Aaron, our head mechanic. We may have a situation here."

"How bad is it?" He asked, bracing himself for the worst.

She looked at Aaron, smirking.

"Well," he answered, "there's a metal zip tie on your crank hub."

With an exasperated sigh, he replied, "That's what I was afraid it would be! How much are we looking at to replace it?"

Her smirk slid into a grin. "We'll be fixing this one on the house, but we want to know how it happened."

"I don't understand."

"This is not a car problem, it's a prankster problem," said Aaron.

As the words sank in, Miles could feel the warm rush of embarrassment rise in his face. *I should have put fruit in his hat! The woodpeckers would have loved that!*

Rylee leaned in. "Aaron and I have an idea."

Miles returned to the waiting room with a stunned look on his face. He sat down quietly and stared back at the door.

"What's wrong?" asked Bill.

Miles slowly turned to him and said, "Someone tried to kill me."

Bewildered, Bill asked, "That's crazy, who would want to kill you?"

"I don't know, but they're calling the police."

Bill turned sideways in his chair to face Miles.

"How...how do you know? What did they say?"

"There's a metal zip tie on the crank hub. If I'd have driven much further, it'd have gummed up the — I can't remember the name of the part. You know I'm no good with cars."

"Nobody dies because of a zip tie on the crank hub!" Bill argued.

"Apparently, people have."

Just then, Rylee opened the door. "Miles, they want to ask you a few questions. Would you like to step outside?" she asked.

Miles turned to Bill as he got up to follow her out the door. "I'll be right back."

Outside and out of sight of the door, Rylee asked, "You guys prank each other a lot? What's your best one?"

Aaron joined them as Miles answered. "To be honest, he's better at it than I am, but I get a good one in once in a while. We make sure they're harmless, just enough to keep us on our toes. It's all in good fun."

As Miles began to relay their storied history, Bill exploded out of the door. His breath short and face sweaty, he explained himself to Rylee and Aaron. "I am so sorry! I thought it was only going to make some noise, I had no idea anything bad could happen, I swear!" He then turned to Miles with tears in his eyes. "I'm so sorry, Miles. I really didn't want to kill you!"

With her ear to the phone, Rylee turned to Miles. "They want to know if you want to press charges."

Struggling to determine whether this had gone too far, Miles considered giving his brother a break. Before he could consciously decide, and much to his dismay, he could not hold back from laughing.

Rylee and Aaron joined him, watching Bill's face go from deep guilt and shock to one of embarrassed relief as the realization hit him — he'd fallen for his own prank. Joining in the laughter, Bill gave Miles a big bear hug and shook Rylee and Aaron's hands. "You got me," he admitted, "You got me good!".

The next morning, Bill knocked on the cabin door. "I was thinking maybe you two would like to go to Falling Rock Cafe over in Munising for breakfast before we all go home. I hear they have some pretty good breakfast burritos."

"One of the other guests was talking about that place. It sounds really good," Rebecca said, coffee in hand. "I'm sure Miles will agree once he's done packing." Seeing him come out of the bedroom with his suitcase, she asked, "Hey, did you guys ever find your bird? I don't remember you saying."

Miles looked at Bill, trying to remember what he saw. With a look of surprised remembrance, he pulled out his phone. Opening the photos app, he clicked on the last picture taken.

The three of them stared at the phone. Miles noticed something in the corner of the screen and enlarged it. Nope, just a yellow streak.

"Well, that's Bill waking up to a very angry blue jay eating out of his hat, and this blue wing is the bird flying away from him. See that little bit of yellow right here? That's the Kirtland's Warbler, I'm sure of it."

"You can't prove that. Wait...What do you mean, eating out of my hat? And how were you able to get that picture so fast?"

Miles looked up at Bill, knowing he was caught. "I'll explain it over breakfast burritos," he muttered. "They're on me, since the car repair bill was so cheap."

Miles did a once-over to make sure they hadn't left anything, when the guest book caught his eye. He knew just what he wanted to write.□

Name: Miles and Rebecca
From: Appleton
Highlight: The Elusive Kirtland's Warbler

The Storm

The snow, coming in sideways with each gust of wind, created bursts of white that were impossible to see through. The windshield wipers had become panicked in their efforts to keep up, and again needed to have the ice snapped from them. The daylight was waning, and with it, Ben's ability to stay on the road. Despite the four-wheel-drive, his tires were starting to spin on developing patches of ice.

A glance in the rearview mirror reminded him of the importance of finding warmth and safety. His son, Sammy, was asleep in the back seat, blissfully unaware of the danger they were in. Desperate, he looked for any kind of shelter he could use to get them through the night. Between bursts of snow, he made out a break in the trees shortly ahead. Although he'd driven this highway many times, he struggled to remember what he would find there. Nothing looked like it normally did in the snowy twilight.

As he got closer, the outline of the small cabins brought back to his memory the resort he'd passed so often. "Looks like we're staying here tonight, Sammy," he announced as he made his best guess where the entrance to the parking lot would be.

He pulled into the lot and tried to make out what he could of the cabins. His hope soared as he saw that one had a fireplace. *Heat!* His mind raced as he tried to figure out how he would cut wood with no ax. Perhaps they would have some already cut, he hoped.

The resort name could still be made out on the sign, but barely. Ben tried calling the number. No answer, just an automated message stating they were closed for the next three weeks. If he wanted to leave a message, the owners would get back to him as soon as they could.

He hung up, clutching the top of the steering wheel with both hands. In his frustration, he leaned his head on the back of his hands.

All I want to do is get my kid to a doctor. Why is this so hard? He had no answers, and no time for self-pity.

He decided to try calling again, this time leaving a message. "Hello...uh...my name is Ben. I'm parked in front of one of your cabins. It looks like...the log one. I'm here with my five-year-old son, and we are stuck in the blizzard. We need shelter, and there's no way I can get anywhere else tonight. I'm not looking to destroy your property, but we need to get inside. I'm just asking that you please not press charges against me for trespassing. If you call me as soon as you get this, we can work out a way for me to pay you for whatever it will cost."

He hung up the phone, deciding he had bigger things to worry about. *I have no idea how to break into a cabin,* he thought, *but I have to figure it out.* Taking a mental inventory of the tools he kept in the back, he formed a plan.

"Hey, Buddy," he said, trying to wake Sammy. "Sam, I need you to listen, ok? I'm going to get out and get us into that cabin over there. I need you to stay in the truck where it's warm until I come and get you, alright?"

The five-year-old sleepily agreed, pulling his blanket up in anticipation of the cold blast of air coming when the truck door opened. Only his eyes showed between the hat and the blanket, and they just didn't want to open.

Ben climbed out of the truck and sank to his knees in the drift of snow. With legs that felt like they were churning cement, he made his way to the front door. Sliding a credit card down the door jamb he desperately tried to remember everything he'd ever heard about picking a lock. He tried all of the easy combinations he could think of on the keypad, but to no avail. It was getting darker, and the temperature was dropping with each blast of cold air coming off the lake. Lumbering back to his truck, he pulled out plan B, a lug wrench.

The keypad acquiesced immediately, giving him access. "Fort Knox it ain't", he mumbled under his breath. Using the flashlight on his phone, he looked around, taking stock of what could be useful as he searched for the circuit breaker. Finding it behind a painting in the bedroom, he held his breath as he flipped the switch. Nothing. His mind raced to figure out why. He then realized that with the resort closed, they may have unplugged everything. With renewed hope, he flipped the light switch. His arm flinched because of the sudden light.

A text notification came through as he walked back into the living room. "MAYO CLINIC: Ben, you have a cardiology visit scheduled for Sammy on 01/23 starting at 2:30 pm. Press 1 to confirm, 2 to reschedule, 3 to cancel." He pressed 1 and waited for the text to show it was confirmed.

He knew he couldn't leave Sammy in the truck alone any longer. Trudging out to the vehicle, he carried his son through the snow drifts and into the cabin.

"It's cold in here, too", Sammy said as he watched the moisture in his breath billow out into the room.

"Give me a minute, I can only work on one thing at a time. I'm going to see if we can use this fireplace. Here, wrap up in some blankets," he said, as he swaddled Sammy in a quilt from the back of the sofa. Sammy giggled at being wrapped up so tight, then complained that his head was still cold. Ben took off his own hat and pulled it over Sammy's head, clear down to his chin. "How's that?" He asked.

"Now I can't see," he said, giggling again.

"Well then, you'll have to wear your own hat." Ben took his hat back and put it on his own head.

"But my arms are stuck."

Ben picked up Sammy to throw him softly on the sofa, making sure he landed just right. He then grabbed the hat his son took off by habit when first entering, and he put it back on Sammy's head. "How about I turn the TV on and you can watch something while I try to figure out the fireplace situation?"

Finding the switch to the fireplace, Ben turned it on. Nothing. He pulled the grate off the bottom and looked for a pilot light, or valve, or anything that could help him get it started. He turned the valve to open and breathed in through his nose. He smelled nothing, which told him the propane had been turned off at the tank.

As he tightened the valve again for safety, a small voice came from the quilt cocoon. "Dad, I have to use the bathroom."

"Well, there's no running water, so we'll have to see what we can do." Ben rummaged around in the kitchen and found a small bucket meant for cleaning. He placed it in the toilet and let Sammy work out the rest. "It all has to land in the bucket. Don't forget to use the hand sanitizer." He pulled a small bottle from his pocket and placed it on the counter.

As he closed the door and walked back to the living room, he heard a faint, "AAAAHH! So cold!"

Chuckling, Ben decided to check in at home. "Hey, Babe, how are you feeling? How's the baby?"

"Mom's barely letting me do anything for her other than feeding, but I'm tired enough that I'm ok with that. Dad's been trying to teach her to say, "Papa".

"A week old is a little early for that, don't you think?"

"Well, he's trying to get a head start. You'll have to make up for it when you get back." Her her tone changed to concern as she continued. "Man, that storm came from nowhere, it's all over the media. Can you even see the roads?"

"I wasn't going to take any chances." Ben gave her the short version, letting her know he had to find the propane tank and charge his phone. "If I can get us going tomorrow before noon, we should still be able to make it in time."

"Sounds good. I'm glad you're off the road for the night. Please be careful, and let us know when you get there."

"I will, thanks. I love you both so much. Give Cassie a kiss for us."

"I love you, too. Give Big Bro Sam a hug and a kiss for us, too."

As he closed his phone, Sammy came out of the bathroom and asked to be rewrapped. Once the boy was rebundled, Ben offered him a cheese stick from the small cooler of snacks they'd brought for their trip. Sammy was still tired, and it was only a matter of minutes, Ben knew, before he'd be sleeping again.

"In order to get the fireplace working, I have to go outside. It might take me a little bit to find the propane tank, so I need you to be brave, ok?"

"Uh huh," Sammy replied, flipping through the channels with the remote.

"Don't play with my phone until I get back. It needs to charge. Once you're done eating, get your hands back in the blanket until I get the heat on, ok?"

"Ok, but are we going to have supper?"

"One thing at a time," Ben answered. "Once I get the heat on, then I'll make us dinner. I think Grandma packed us some meals for the hotel. We can eat them tonight instead. I think there might even be some hot dogs, but they're still in the bigger cooler in the truck."

"They'd be cold dogs in here," Sammy said.

"Not for long, your DAD's on it!" Ben announced in a superhero voice, flexing his biceps. He then put his gloves on with similar vigor and stomped like a giant to the front door. Before opening it, he turned and calmly reassured his son. "Love you, Buddy. I'll be back in a few."

"Love you, too, Dad!" Sammy shouted through the cheese stick in his mouth.

Ben's smile fell as he exited the cabin. He'd already taught his son some very important things for a young boy to know; how to catch a fish, how to tie a variety of knots, and how and when to call 911. He hoped that last one would never be needed.

The old cabin was drafty, and Ben knew it was only a matter of time before the blankets wouldn't be enough. He needed to find the propane tank, and he needed to do it quickly. From his truck, he pulled an emergency shovel and a visor light, which he attached to the baseball cap he found under the backseat. He then put the baseball cap under his knit cap and turned the light on. Like the street lamp in the parking lot, it lit up mostly blowing snow, but was somewhat reassuring. While he was thinking of it, Ben decided to slide the large cooler to rest just inside the door for later.

Clicking his visor light off, his eyes adjusted to see further in the dark without the light reflecting on the flying snowflakes. He could see little, however, and nothing that looked like a propane tank. The best odds were behind the cabin. Walking carefully through the snowbank, he used his shovel to knock the drift down to a height his legs could navigate. His arms and thighs burned from the strain, but he rounded the corner hopeful.

More snow, no tank. Dropping his shoulders, he took a deep breath and looked again. The ice forming on his eyelashes, along with the snow in his face, was making it difficult to see anything. He pulled his hand out of his glove to melt the frozen droplets from his lashes and to wipe his eyes. Opening them again, he struggled to figure out if the shape before him was shadow or substance. As his eyes adjusted, his hope returned. Sticking out of the snowbank about 15 feet from him was the end of a propane tank. Adrenaline rushed through his body as he put in an all-out slow motion run through the snow. "Woo hoo!" he yelled. Heat was near at hand!

Ben stood the shovel in the snow and used his arms to clear the top. He flipped the cover and opened the valve. Laughing victoriously, he pictured the fuel flowing through the pipes to the cabin. *Finally, something is going right!*

Catching one boot on the other while trying to maneuver the 180-degree turn, he lost his balance. There was nothing to grab onto for stability, and the foot carrying his weight slid forward, reeling him backwards. The cold metal tank slammed the back of his head, causing him to see stars as he hit the snow.

His eyes still closed, Ben did a systems check of his body. His legs hurt, but they still worked, as did his feet. Hands and arms? Check. Neck and head? No answer. How long had he been laying there? He had no idea.

He was sleepy and a little dizzy, which worried him. Not knowing how long he'd been out, he had no idea how cold Sammy would be. He needed to get back to the cabin as quickly as possible, concussion or not. The fireplace still needed to be started, and Sam wouldn't know how to work it.

Carefully, he moved to sit up. Slowly, he half walked and half crawled toward the back of the cabin, where the underside of the snow drift would make an easier route. A few steps toward it, he had to stop to wait for the dizziness to subside. It didn't. Knowing what was coming, he dropped to his knees and made a hole in the snow in front of him. Nausea gave way to vomiting, which left him even more weak. He slid snow over the hole to cover the smell, and waited to get his strength back.

This is too much for any man. The dizziness overcame him again and he rolled to his side. His head stung as it hit the snow. Ben had been through hard things. He lost his dad when he was twelve, and he'd been living through five years of a child with a birth defect in his heart. Sammy was worth the stress, but it was still hard. And now, just days after their daughter was born, he is stuck in a blizzard, trying to get his son to one of the few specialists in the country that can help him. The tears came slowly at first, but quickly turned to full-on sobs, and the stress made it's way out of his body. He was left exhausted, but the time to let it out was not wasted. With the emotional release came renewed vigor.

This is not how this ends, he told himself. Ben drew a deep breath and clawed his way through the drift to the underside next to the back wall of the cabin. From there, he crawled along the side of the cabin until he got back to the porch, each crawling step bringing more determination to reach his goal.

He worried about scaring Sammy by crawling into the cabin with a blood on his hands and head. Mustering all of his remaining strength and using the railing, he stood upright. It took an awkward moment to catch his balance, but once he did, he was able to venture up the two steps, albeit slowly, and then to the front door.

As he opened the door, he noticed the TV was muted. Sammy was talking on the phone. "My dad's back, do you want to talk to him?"

"Who is it?" Ben asked.

"He's the owner." Sammy answered, his arm with the phone sticking out of the blanket cocoon.

"I gotta light the fireplace, ask him to hang on." Ben thought for a moment, remembering the lighter on the table. Deciding to bring it just in case, he stumbled to the fireplace.

"Are you ok, Dad?" Sammy asked, concerned.

"I'll be ok, I just hit my head. Just...just give me a minute."

"He's gotta light the fireplace, he'll talk to you in a minute," Sammy repeated into the phone. With the discretion common to many a five-year-old, he added, "He hit his head, so it might be a minute."

"Is he ok?" Asked the voice on the other side.

"He'll be ok. He said to give him a minute."

The click of the lighter and a whoosh of the flames gave Ben the reassurance he needed. Still weak, he sat down. The heat from the fire didn't take long to warm the air near it.

"Dad, the guy wants to talk to you," reminded Sammy.

"Come here, Sammy, sit by the fire with me," Ben said. "Bring the phone."

Sammy dropped the phone trying to wriggle back out of his blanket. After finding it again, he grabbed the blanket and came over to sit next to Ben on the hearth, handing him the phone.

"Hello?"

"Hello, this is Kristofer. My wife and I run the resort. Your son was telling me about your situation. I don't want you worrying about the door."

"Thank you," Ben's thoughts were becoming foggy, his head throbbing.

"Do I understand correctly, you hit your head?"

"While I was turning on the propane at the tank. The snow was deep and..." his voice trailed off while he tried to pull his emotions together.

"I have a neighbor that can get there quickly with his snowmobile. His name's Danny, he used to be a nurse. I'll be sending him over to make sure you're both ok."

"I think I'm ok, I just need some rest."

"Yeah, that's not a good idea. Don't sleep until Danny can get there. I'm calling him now. You said you're in the log cabin?"

"Yes, I think it was cabin 2?"

"I'll send him right over."

Ben thanked him again and hung up the phone. "I know you're still cold, Sammy, but can you help me get my boots off, please? I'm not feeling very good. Be careful, the floor's wet over here." He gestured toward the newly melting snow coming from his shoes and jeans.

Sammy untied the boots and pulled off the first one. "Oooh, stinky," he teased, "You've got stinky feet!" He waved his hand in front of his face, pretending to be offended.

"Not as stinky as yours!" Ben managed to get out, making every effort to maintain a sense of normalcy. "I'll bet you can't get the second one off. You're not strong enough, are you?" Talking getting hard.

Sammy was eager to prove himself strong, which he did to the delight of them both. Ben cheered softly, his feet finally getting some of the warmth coming from the fireplace.

The sound of snowmobiles getting closer signaled help coming, and Ben asked Sammy to open the door for them. As he did, two people dressed in snowmobile suits and helmets entered the room. The first held a medical kit. Stomping their boots and closing the door, they took off their helmets. "Hello. I'm Danny, and this is my wife, Meghan. You must be Ben."

Ben grimaced at the stomping sounds, then nodded.

"May I take a look at your head?"

"I would appreciate that."

While Danny examined Ben, Meghan asked Sammy if he'd eaten.

"I had some cheese sticks when we first got here. Dad was going to make dinner, but then he hit his head."

"What was he going to make, do you know?"

"Hot dogs."

"Well, it just so happens that I know how to make hot dogs. Would they be in that cooler over there?"

Turning to Ben, she asked, "Is it ok if I..."

"Do whatever you need to," Ben answered.

"I'm afraid Ben will have to hold off for a while on eating," explained Danny, helping him to the sofa. "You may have a concussion." The look on his face as he spoke to Ben showed the concern he didn't want Sammy to notice. Lowering his voice, he added, "Under normal circumstances, I'd take you to the hospital to have some imaging tests done as a precaution, but we may have to wait on that until morning."

"I'm sure I'll be fine. I'm not hungry anyway, so go ahead and eat, Sammy. You must be starving." He paused for a moment, overwhelmed.

"I wasn't sure I needed you to come, but now that you're here, I'm so glad you did. Between the head injury and Sammy, I wasn't sure which of us was going to be taking care of which."

"Well, get used to us. We're not leaving you alone here," Meghan said, putting some hot dogs in the microwave.

"I understand you boys were on your way to Rochester?" Danny asked.

"We were, until the storm changed directions." He leaned back, holding the cold pack on the back of his head. The irony of still feeling cold from the snow and adding a cold pack was not lost on him. The cold pack was, however, dulling the pain.

As Sammy enjoyed his hot dogs and a juice box, Danny helped Ben get into some dryer clothes. Meghan sat at the table with her back to them, giving Ben the privacy he needed. Now in sweatpants and a button up shirt, Ben explained Sammy's heart condition, their newborn baby, and moving in with his in-laws to make it all work. "We just couldn't do it all alone. Grandma and Grandpa have been amazing, right Sammy?"

"Right! Grandpa's gonna take me ice fishing!"

"That sounds like fun!" Meghan said before turning to Ben. "When is the appointment in Rochester?"

"At 2:30 on the 23rd. We left a day early on purpose. Unfortunately, the storm took that from us. Now if I can't drive..." Ben paused for a moment, trying to collect his thoughts. Despite his best attempts to hold it together, the desperation came through in his voice. "The doctor we're seeing is booked up for months in advance, and he had a cancellation. We can't wait months. We have to get there."

Danny looked at Meghan. "I think I can pull some strings and get the scans of your head done tomorrow morning. If they can clear you for driving, you can be on your way. If not...well, we'll make sure you get there."

Early the next morning, Ben woke up to the sound of a snowmobile starting and then leaving. The bright sunlight poured in through the windows, signaling an end to the blizzard and the beginning of a deep cold snap. The smell of coffee lingered in the air as Ben groggily sat up. He touched his head, wondering if the bump had gone down. It had. The sound of snow plows gave Ben renewed hope of reaching Rochester by 2:30 after all.

"Good morning," said Danny quietly, "How do you feel?"

"I have a bad headache, but the dizziness is gone. Where's Sammy?"

"Still sleeping. It's not even six." Danny walked around behind him to check the back of his head. "You seem to be improving, but we'll need imaging done before you can get behind the wheel of a car."

Ben nodded in agreement, reluctantly.

"They'll check you out as soon as we can get you to the hospital."

Ben slowly got up, his body as achy and stiff as the day after a car accident. "Where's um..."

"Meghan. She went to get our truck. You can't drive right now."

Sammy entered the kitchen, his hair disheveled to an extreme degree, even for him.

Ben chuckled softly at the sight. "We're going to be leaving soon, Buddy. Get your clothes on, ok? Danny brought your backpack in from the truck last night."

"What about breakfast?"

"While your dad's getting checked out at the hospital, we'll go to the cafeteria. I heard they have waffles today." Danny answered.

Sammy's eyes lit up, and he darted back to the bedroom with his backpack to change.

By the time he was finished, Meghan showed up with the truck.

Danny explained, "If you're ok with me driving your truck, we can follow Meghan. If you're ok to drive, you can be on your way, and if not, we can leave your truck there and we can take the two of you to Rochester and back."

"After all you've done for us, you can drive my truck any time you want," Ben said, handing him the keys.

While Meghan waited in their vehicle, Danny started loading up their things.

"What is this book?" asked Sammy. "I can't read it."

"Bring it over here, please," Ben said as he put on his boots.

Sammy handed him the guestbook.

"It's a book people sign. You can't read it because it's in cursive."

"Why do people sign it? What's it for?"

"It lets us see what kind of fun other people had when they stayed here. For example, here's one. Chris V from Marshfield says his highlight was 'One very, very good dog'. What do you think happened there?"

"I don't know," Sammy answered, shrugging. "Maybe he knows how to fish!" They laughed. "I think all dogs are good," he said. "Unless they're bad, though..."

"I'd agree with that," Danny said, "same as people."

"So, what should we say?" Sammy asked.

"Well, we're not really... ah...maybe we should say something," Ben answered.

"I'll get a pen," Sammy replied.□

Name: Sammy and Ben
From: Escanaba
Highlight: The kindness of strangers

New Shoes

A iden knew that look, but didn't expect it here. Savannah, his wife, was admiring a small painting hung on the wall of the cabin, scrutinizing its details. He watched as she squinted and stepped closer, then pulled her head back, trying to make out the signature.

"I don't recognize the name," she lamented, "but it's quite good. Do you have the phone number for the hosts? I'd like to ask them about the artist".

Aiden looked at the painting himself. What he saw was an impressionist piece of a lake scene on an 8x10 canvas with a cheap wooden frame. While it was aesthetically pleasing, he had no sense of what would categorize a work of art as 'fine'. He usually based his judgement on the quality of the frame and the price on the tag, leaving the rest up to his wife.

Savannah, however, had exquisite taste, and he could read her. He loved watching the gears in her head turn. When she was deeply interested, she could stare at a piece for some time.

Having been there an entire fifteen minutes, it seemed too long for him to not have seen the lakeshore that would define their weekend. "Perhaps we can check with them tomorrow? Let's go down to the lake and see the view, shall we?"

Reluctantly, she accepted his invitation. She knew she needed the break from work, but couldn't help contemplating the details of the painting while she put her shoes back on. After grabbing her sweatshirt, she walked with him down the winding path to the sand. The crisp autumn air was ideal, and their trip to the cabin felt like entering another world. While all of the Great Lakes cool the cities that lie against them, Michigan was no match for the cooling power of Superior. At home in Milwaukee, it was still in the 80s and everything was green. Here, the leaves were changing, though not quite at their peak. The bright sun lit up the trees like bouquets of stained glass against a bright blue sky, bringing her into her favorite time o f year.

They put a blanket on the ground and sat next to each other as they took in the view of the water. "Please don't let me forget to find out about that artist, will you?" she asked.

"Of course, not," Aiden responded, knowing he would forget long before she would.

While architecture is considered an art form by some, Aiden felt it was more of a skill. He loved the problem-solving part the most, delighting clients with remodeling ideas and fixes that went well beyond their requests. Had it not been for a few of those clients' suggestions to go out on his own, as well as Savannah's unwavering support, he'd never have taken the risk.

For that reason alone, Aiden would make sure she found out the name of the artist, even if it took up a chunk of their weekend together. He wanted to be equally supportive of her career, and as the new gallerist for one of the most up-and-coming galleries of the Milwaukee area, she took her work and her artists very seriously. It was one of the things he appreciated about her. As a young career couple, they were seeing their dreams come true.

A threatening dark cloud loomed over him, though. No matter how beautiful the lake was, nor how bright their future looked, it could all come crashing down at any moment, and he was struggling to make sure

Savannah didn't feel it. The sound of the waves rolling in and the fresh water scent offered to many a tourist a line of demarcation between the world they needed a vacation from and the world where they vacationed. Today, the lake gave Aiden no such solace.

He was twelve years old when the man he felt could do no wrong died. Having been of the belief that doctors were only for sick people, Grandpa Jack wasn't diagnosed until he was having a hard time breathing. The family assumed it was lung cancer until the test results came back as testicular. By then, there was little to be done.

"You look pretty sad for someone who's on vacation." Savannah's voice jolted him back to the present day. "What's on your mind?"

"I was just thinking about Grandpa Jack," he answered, wishing he could think of anything else right now.

She nodded as if she understood, and put her head on his shoulder.

Knowing she didn't, Aiden smirked and put his arm around her. He hoped she never would. Together, they sat in silence, watching the waves while his mind drifted back to where he'd left off.

Thankfully, Aiden's father chose not to follow in his father's viewpoints on healthcare. He made sure Aiden and his brothers were well-educated in what to watch for and what to do if they started seeing the signs. His father's urgency in getting care quickly ran through his mind as he remembered noticing the lump in the shower. He was tested the day before they left, and the results could be back at any time. He wanted to wait to find out for sure before putting Savannah through the emotional rollercoaster. She had so much on her mind already with the new job, and there was nothing to do about it but wait anyway. With little time to research the latest treatments and prognosis, Aiden decided to leave that rabbit hole alone until he knew it contained a rabbit.

Deciding to focus on something — anything — else, he turned his attention to asking his wife out for dinner.

The next morning, Aiden left a note on the table saying he was running to get some good coffee in Marquette, and would be back soon. He needed time to process his circumstances without chance of interruption. Since Savannah was still tired from the emotional investment in a recent gallery show, it seemed a good time for him to get time alone and do something nice for her at the same time. After a few minutes of driving, though, he again decided to put off going down that rabbit hole. Instead, he decided to make a phone call to track down the artist of the painting in the cabin.

Returning to the cabin with coffee and two very large and beautiful blueberry muffins in hand, he was eager to talk about the bakery he'd found. While still at Babycakes, he decided to take a croissant for the road, as he was quite hungry, and unsure how long Savannah would sleep. If the muffins were anywhere as good as the croissant, he knew he'd made the right choice.

Setting the coffee and muffins on the table, he went into the bedroom. Her face no longer looked as peaceful as when he'd left. "Hon, would you like some coffee? I also got some blueberry muffins...fresh baked today," he said gently, sitting on the bed next to her.

She sat up suddenly, still sleepy, with the color draining from her face. "I don't feel very good," she grumbled. "Can you help me to the bathroom?"

They got there just in time for her to get rid of her dinner from the night before. He gave her water, a cool washcloth and mouthwash to refresh herself, then asked if she preferred to sit in the living room or stay where she was.

"I think there might have been something wrong with the ribs I had last night," she lamented.

"I think you should lie down and get some rest," he said. "Let me help you back to bed." He felt her forehead for signs of a fever, but found none. "Here's a small trash can, just in case you can't make it to the bathroom next time. Maybe you'll start feeling better now that you got rid of it."

"I hope so. Maybe I just need some more sleep."

"I have some ginger ale with us. Would you like to sip on that?"

"Sure," she said groggily, "maybe that will help."

By the time he returned with the can of soda from the kitchen, she was snoring quietly. He decided to leave her where she was for the time being, and headed out to the living area to give her some space.

Everything about this weekend was going wrong. They'd planned it nearly a month ago, knowing she'd need the break after the last gallery night. They didn't plan on food poisoning, nor was he planning on waiting for life-changing test results. Neither was conducive to relaxing, or to the bonding time they so desperately needed.

He decided to turn on the television softly and enjoy his muffin. He wondered how food could make one person sick but not another. What did she eat that he didn't? She had the coleslaw. *Probably the mayonnaise,* he decided. Maybe it sat out too long? Either way, there was nothing to be done except to wait it out and make sure she was improving.

Somewhere around mid-morning, Savannah got up and came out of the bedroom. Not wanting to overtax her, Aiden asked what she felt like doing.

"I wanted to go for a hike through the woods, but I'm not sure I'm up to it. Could we go into town and do some exploring? My mind needs stimulation, but my body is pretty wiped from earlier." Her face lit up as she saw the muffin he'd brought for breakfast. "Ooh, is this for me? It looks amazing."

"It is amazing, and it's yours. I tried to give it to you earlier, but the timing wasn't so good. If you think your stomach can handle it, I'll warm it up in the microwave for you."

As she gratefully savored the warm blueberry goodness, he regaled her with his morning experience. He gave her the artist's information, texted to him by the resort owner. "They checked with her before passing her information along, and she was thrilled you took notice of it."

"Well, I can tell you, she's got a place in the gallery if she wants it. That is, if her other pieces are as good. Would you mind if I called her quickly to see if she has time to show us some other pieces? I know we're on vacation, but..."

"Don't worry about it, that sounds great to me. Maybe we could meet with her over lunch if she's able?"

Savannah and Aiden met with the artist at a small cafe. The young woman, Eleanora, came with a large shopping bag full of her favorite works on canvas. "I'm sorry, I don't really have a proper portfolio, I never expected this. These are the ones my parents had on display." She bit her bottom lip as she pulled one onto her lap. Her eyes darted from Savannah to Aiden and back again as she turned the canvas around. "This one is the one I am most proud of. It's a view of my great-grandparent's farm."

Savannah began with an encouraging smile, then looked the painting over. "Your work is very good. Would you be interested in allowing me to hang some of these in a gallery in Milwaukee?"

By the look on her face, Eleanora was still having a hard time believing this was happening to her. "Are you sure? I mean, I would be honored!" Her face quickly turned to careful curiosity as she asked, "What would I have to do? Would I need to pay for that?"

"There's a whole packet of information I can email you as to how the process works. You would pay nothing up front, but we do get a commission from your sales. Here's my business card. If you'd like, I can send you the information and then give you a few days to go through it. Would you be available for a video call on Friday? I can show you around the gallery and explain our upcoming events."

Eleanora, a home health aide whose parents owned the resort, thought her parents were trying to save money by decorating the cabins with her paintings. That, or they were trying to encourage to her to keep working on her skills. Either way, painting was therapeutic for her. After a long day of caring for those who were suffering, the paintings helped to remind her of the beautiful things in life.

The more Savannah talked, the more Eleanora felt she could sell the paintings. As Savannah knew all too well, a large part of appreciating a painting is appreciating the one who painted it. Marketing an artist's personality along with the pieces can drive up the price.

Eleanora nearly tripped on her way out the door, eager to tell her parents and friends what just happened. The couple, amused by her excitement, watched her until she got in her car, then walked in the opposite direction.

"Eleanora is such a beautiful name," Savannah observed.

"And what a lovely personality to go with it," Aiden agreed. "For a moment, I was worried she was going to pass out. Are they always like this?"

"Sometimes. Other times, their ego is better than their work."

His phone rang, and he signaled to Savannah that he would need a moment of privacy. She nodded and stepped inside a nearby gift shop.

"I usually prefer to have these discussions in person," his doctor flatly stated.

"I can take whatever the answer is, I just need to know what I'm dealing with," Aiden said.

"It's in the early stages, and there are a lot of treatment options with good results. I have an appointment already made for you with the best oncologist I know. You can cancel it and choose your own, of course, but he had a rare opening due to a cancellation, so I took it on your behalf."

After a few more questions, Aiden put the appointment in his calendar and thanked the doctor for the information and the appointment. He thought about how odd it was that he felt shock, as he already knew the results were a strong possibility. The feelings were more overwhelming than he'd imagined. He put his head in his hands, suddenly understanding Grandpa Jack's decision to live in denial.

He then called to mind the efforts of his father to save him from the results of ignoring it. He couldn't help but be grateful for his dad's persistance, and the kind and optimistic words of his doctor.

"There you are!" Savannah cheerfully walked toward him as she came out of the gift shop carrying a gift bag. "Are you finished with..."

He raised his head, knowing the look on his face would stop her short, but being unable to hide it from her any longer. "I'll be ok, just need to process some news. Nothing to worry about right now. How about we head back?"

"Would you like me to drive?" she asked.

"No, I'm...I'm ok," he answered, trying to maintain a semblance of normalcy. The shock was wearing off, and he was confident he could distract himself mentally until they returned to the cabin. As they walked back to the car, he felt his equilibrium return.

He knew she would be there for him, of that there was no doubt. But how would this affect her? How would she take the news? His thoughts raced. As he felt his emotional balance sway, he decided a conversation would help.

"So, what did you find at the gift shop?" he asked.

Savannah had just checked the notification coming in on her phone, and his question surprised her. She looked up as she answered. "Uh...a box."

"You bought a box?"

"Yes. It's a wooden one, and it's all hand carved and amazingly beautiful. I can't wait to show you when we get back!" Her enthusiasm for a box was infectious, and he found himself intrigued.

"The lady at the counter wrapped it like we were throwing it in a moving truck," she continued. "But at least it'll be perfect when we get it home."

"Well, that sounds nice. Where will you put it?"

"I was thinking on the mantel."

"This must be some box." He was now curious as to what kind of carving would make a wooden box worthy of a place on their mantel.

As he put the car in park in front of the cabin, the sky let loose a deluge of rain. The sheer timing was so incredulous that Aiden burst forth in laughter.

Savannah chuckled, but couldn't see the level of humor Aiden found in the rainstorm. As his laughter subsided, tears welled up in his eyes. He knew she would not buy that they were tears of laughter, but he didn't know how to express in words what he was feeling.

"Aiden, we're here now. What is it? What has happened?"

He paused, trying to figure out where to start. He decided to get it all out in one breath. He watched as the weight of his words sank in. "I went to the doctor on Thursday morning. The phone call was from my doctor. Savannah...I have cancer."

"What?" she asked in a whisper.

The sooner he could get her through the hard part and onto the hopeful part, the better. With this in mind, he turned toward her as much as the steering wheel would allow and took her hand. "Savannah, I have testicular cancer. It's in the early stages, and there are a lot of things they can do, but I don't know much more yet. I have an appointment with a very highly recommended oncologist on Tuesday. I have no idea how my doctor got me in so quickly, but he did."

Aiden warned her while they were dating that this was a possibility, and she knew enough to know it likely wasn't fatal. She also knew enough to know it wasn't going to be easy.

"I...I..." was all she could stammer out.

"I'm so sorry," he said, realizing how this would affect their careers, their finances, and everything they were planning. The tears again welled up in his eyes.

"There's no reason to be sorry," she blurted with an anxious chuckle. "Why didn't you tell me you were going in? I would've been there for you."

"I was hoped it would be negative, and I wouldn't have to worry you about it. You needed to focus on the gallery."

She leaned over to hug him. With her forehead touching his and her hand on his shoulder, she declared, "No job will ever be as important as you are. We are a team. You can't just bench me like that. From now on, we have to be in this together."

He sheepishly agreed, but was more comforted than he thought he would be at her support. The tears fell as he began to tell her his symptoms, the appointment, and the resulting phone call. Reassuring her of his chances of survival helped to reassure him, and together they created a plan of action that would cover how they would deal with whatever treatment was needed.

An hour went by quickly, and they finally decided to go inside. Neither was hungry for a big meal, so they decided to make sandwiches from the chicken salad they brought and add a side of chips for dinner. They sat on a rug in front of the fireplace to eat. A clean towel acted as a make-shift picnic blanket.

"Babe," he said quietly, "what if we can't have children?"

Savannah's jaw dropped. "Is...is that a concern?"

"I don't know, but I'll ask the oncologist."

"You mean WE'LL ask the oncologist. We're in this together, remember? We're Team Aiden". She gasped as she remembered the box. "Speaking of Team Aiden...would you like to see the box?"

"Of course! If it's going on our mantel, it must be some box."

After going to the car to grab the bag she'd forgotten, she handed him the well-wrapped box.

He struggled to pull the shipping tape from the cardboard outer layer without damaging the contents, and finally pulled out his pocket knife . He carefully sliced the tape to open the cardboard. "You're right, we could drop this off a cliff and it'd be unharmed." Eventually, he was able to get the wooden box out of the bubble wrapped inner layer. "Wow, this is really nice. Is it hand carved?" He asked, looking at the detail and trying to discern the type of wood grain he was seeing. "Is it walnut?"

"It's both," she replied, "but that's not the present...it's just the box."

"There's more?" He wondered aloud, looking at her as he flipped up the latch and opened the top.

"Much more."

The look on her face as she said it took him aback. When he looked down, time seemed to freeze. He had to force himself to breathe again, and as he did, more tears burst forth. Twice in one day, life had him in tears.

Inside the box was the most beautiful and perfect pair of white shoes he had ever seen. Together they could fit in the palm of one of his hands. The words fought over themselves trying to leave his mouth. "Are...are you...are we?"

"I am pregnant, and we are both healthy."

Savannah's reassuring smile helped him absorb the news. He could feel expressions of shock and awe take their turns crossing his face as the day's events spun in his head. After what felt like an eternity, he gained control of himself and rolled onto his knees to hug her, not wanting to let go. As he held her, the day's events started falling together. "It wasn't the ribs, then?".

"No, it wasn't," Savannah said. "Would you like to say, 'Hello'?" She leaned back on her hands, stretching her torso to make their first conversation easier.

What was once an abstract idea of fatherhood now held a place in the real world. He leaned forward and spoke gently to her not-yet-showing belly. "Hey, little one. I'm your Dad. I can't wait to see you, but for now, just do whatever you gotta do in there to be healthy, ok? And I'll do whatever I can to be healthy, too, ok?" He paused to wipe a tear from his eye. "You got it pretty good, little one, because already you have the best mom in the whole world!"

The next morning, Aiden called the resort owners to ask for a delayed check-out. He explained Savannah's condition and her morning sickness, to which Ingrid offered her hearty congratulations and all the time they needed. They'd been awake late into the evening planning a nursery, discussing schools, and even considering names. They were able to decide on a boy's name almost immediately, but a girl's name seemed harder to narrow down.

Today, he could do nothing for his cancer. That was anxiety for another day. Today, his job was to be a doting husband and father, and to be grateful for the opportunity to be one. A stop at *Babycakes* for more muffins along the way had already been requested and promised.

The car was loaded by the time she was done getting dressed, with a ginger ale in her cupholder, just in case. She was feeling well enough to be on their way, but he didn't want to take any chances. He pulled a couple of slices of bread from the loaf in the car and put them in the toaster for her.

While the bread was toasting, she mused at his nurturing side. She pictured him holding their child, and nearly teared up thinking about what he would be like as a father. There would be many days ahead that would be about the baby. Today, she wanted to just enjoy her time with him. "Perhaps we could walk up to the shoreline one more time before we leave?" she asked. "I'd like to get a picture of us at the water. Maybe we could get one of us holding the shoes?"

"That sounds like a great idea," he answered as she checked the rooms for anything they may have forgotten. "I think I have everything except your purse in the car, so we can go ahead and let them know we're done in here." He handed her the toast, wrapped neatly in a paper towel version of a to-go container.

She thanked him, then walked to the end table. "So, what should we say in this guest book? It asks for our names, which city and state we're from, and the highlight of our trip."□

Name: Aiden and Savannah
(and either Johnathan Aiden or Jacqueline Eleanora)
City: Milwaukee, WI□
Highlight: New shoes

The Deep Blue Horizon

E xcited by the peanut he'd stolen from a nearby bird feeder, the small black squirrel stopped in the middle of Kate's path, frozen.

"Hello," she said softly as she stopped, hoping to not scare him away.

He knew he was caught red-handed, but was undeterred. He shoved the entire shell in his mouth, daring her to prove his guilt.

She broke eye contact, letting him off the hook, but only for a moment. Her eyes followed him as he flicked his tail and scampered to the back side of a neighboring tree trunk, victorious but still wary. He peeked his head around the trunk, wanting to reassure himself that she was not coming after his treasure.

"You can keep your peanut," she assured him, chuckling as she continued on the path toward the lakeshore.

The lake is generally at its most hospitable in August, and today Kate availed herself of that hospitality by running headlong into the waves. She let the chilly water take her back to her first summer here as a young girl. A week-long stay in paradise for her family soon became an annual tradition that outlived her parents. These waters had become a symbol of peace and healing in her life, and submerging herself in them had a restorative effect.

Wiping the water from her face as she stood again, Kate surveyed the shoreline. Not much had changed in those decades. The ten cabins, still white with red roofs, were connected by the winding path through the park-like grounds. A single log cabin in the distance remained, the steadfast remnant of a mysterious past.

When she could no longer stand the cold, she walked back up to the beach. Unlike her run toward the water, she now carefully chose her steps to avoid the stones. Once ashore, she grabbed a towel and sat on her blanket to dry her long white hair.

"You are very brave," said a soft voice behind her. "I don't know if I could go in without a wet suit. It's just so cold."

"Depends on what you're comparing it to," Kate said while donning a zip-up sweatshirt and pants over her swimsuit. "August is about as warm as it gets. At my age, I'm rarely comfortable anyway, so I figured I might as well have the adventure." Kate turned her head toward the woman to see her reaction. Instead, what she saw made her laugh. "I guess you know what I'm talking about!"

"I do! I'm also rarely comfortable. And," she added, gesturing toward her very round belly, "I am in for quite an adventure."

"Yes, you are! How close are you?" Kate asked.

Like many before her, the woman had been asked this series of questions enough to automatically recited the answers. "October 20th. He'll be our first. So far, he's healthy and all is good."

"Glad you're getting a vacation now then. Had three of my own. Best thing I ever did was raise good people, and I've done a lot of other fun things. My name's Kate, by the way."

"Hello Kate, I'm Maria," she said. "Do you have grandchildren, too?"

"Four of them, ranging from fifteen to seven, the seven-year-olds being twins." She looked around, as if to find the missing piece of a puzzle, then leaned forward, nearly whispering. "Are you here alone?"

"My husband and I are here together. He's in an interview at the university as we speak, hoping to land a position as an Associate Professor."

"Well, that's a lot going on at once. Where are you from?"

Maria looked down at her hands thoughtfully, then back at Kate. "The LA area. We took a week to get here, stopping to sightsee along the way. I know people do it all the time, but I just dreaded flying pregnant."

"No wonder the water here seems so cold to you! It must seem downright frigid. But hey, at least there aren't any sharks, right?"

"That is what I've been told," Maria said with a smile.

Kate looked thoughtful for a moment, then said, "That's a long time to be in a car for a job he doesn't have yet. He must be feeling a lot of pressure to get it."

"He does have a teaching offer from an online school who is willing to wait to see how this goes. Either way, we're not going back."

"Well, having a back up plan takes the pressure off."

"All the pressure except *this* looming deadline I'm carrying around," she said, gesturing toward the baby. "I've hit the nesting mode with nowhere to apply the instincts." Leaning forward slightly, as if telling some great secret, she said, "It's more of a problem than you'd think."

Kate also leaned forward, as if to show she would keep this secret. "I'm sure it is," she said as she grabbed a pen and sticky note from her bag. "My first daughter slept in a box in my room for weeks until I had a proper crib for her." Her face turned more serious as she continued. "You'd think nine months would be enough time to get ready for a baby, but sometimes...it's just not. Here's my name and phone number. Call me if you need anything, and I mean that. My husband and his brother are out on the water, fishing – will be all week. I just wanted to come along and enjoy the sand and sunshine while they're doing their thing. You won't be interrupting anything if you need some help, and I could use the company anyway."

"Thank you, that's very thoughtful." Maria tucked the paper carefully into the book she'd been reading, using it as a bookmark. "It is nice to have backup, especially since Ansel is going to be starting – well, if he gets the job, anyway – at the beginning of the semester. They're hiring this position a bit late, so he'll be scrambling to get things ready."

"You said he would be an Associate Professor, right? Which department?"

"That's right. Sociology."

"That sounds fascinating."

Maria nodded, smiling. "It does lend itself to some interesting dinner conversations."

"I'll bet it does. Do you have movers coming then?"

"Once we have somewhere to put our things. My sister agreed to come and help us get the smaller stuff settled in a couple of weeks. I can't tell you how much I appreciate that."

"Oh, absolutely!" Kate struggled to not overstep, but her motherly concern pushed her to ask further. "Are your parents able to come too?"

"My sister is the only one capable of helping." Maria answered flatly.

Kate zipped up her sweatshirt as she accepted the boundary. "Then I'm glad you have your sister. It's nice to have someone who knows where you'd want your things to go."

"It is," agreed Maria. She looked out over the water, searching for a change of subject. "The horizon is such a beautiful deep blue today. I really love that color. It's so peaceful looking."

"I've been to all the Great Lakes," replied Kate. "Even though the color of the water changes with the weather, there's a different... something... about their color of blue on a beautiful day that seems to be unique to each of them."

"Which is your favorite?" asked Maria.

"This one. I'm probably biased, though, my family has come here nearly every year since I was a child."

"This is the first time I've seen any of them in person, but from my research, I think this will be my favorite as well."

"Anything in particular that draws you to it?"

"A couple of things, actually. As far as the Great Lakes in general, there are few lakes in the world large enough to change the weather. In some ways, they are similar to small oceans, and other ways to more average-sized lakes, which is very unique. The biological diversity, though, that's the treasure trove I'm interested in. Lake Erie may be the most diverse, but I would love to learn more about a particular type of lake trout that only lives here."

"You have done your research, I'm impressed. Did you know the lake trout can live to a hundred, and have been around since the dinosaurs? That usually impresses the tourists."

"One of the things that fascinate me about them. Such a cool lake, with so many secrets in it."

"One could call it 'great', even," said Kate.

Maria chuckled and nodded as she grabbed the arms of her chair. In one motion, she swung forward and used all four appendages to bring herself to a standing position. Stretching her back, she asked, "By any chance, would you mind watching my things for a moment? I just need to run back to use the bathroom."

"An occupational hazard," said Kate. "Not a problem, I'll be here for a while. Take your time."

As Maria walked away, Kate took a drink from her water bottle and dug a hole in the sand to set the bottle into, convinced it would help keep it cool longer.

The blanket, now warmed in the sun, invited her for a quick rest. She closed her eyes and let her tension melt.

"Kate, guess what?" She heard Maria exclaim as she returned.

Kate rolled over to address her. "He got the job," she said, smiling.

"Not yet, but they're giving him a tour of the campus, so that sounds positive, right?" Her face showed the desperate hope she felt.

"Sure does!"

"Good, I was hoping I wasn't reading into anything." Maria placed a cushion on the chair and resumed her spot, sipping thoughtfully on a fresh lemonade. She looked down at the baby inside of her and then to Kate. "You said you had three kids, right?"

"I did."

"Did you, ah...have any issues?"

Kate smiled. Every pregnant woman has a moment when the reality of labor and delivery hits her, and she knew that moment when she saw it. She also knew the concern had to be met honestly or not at all. "I did. In fact, the last one was an emergency C-section. But you know what? I'm still here, and so is my baby. He's 41 this month, and as healthy as a horse." She made sure Maria was looking at her as she continued. "Modern medicine has a lot of tricks up it's sleeve. You'll be ok — you both will."

"I really appreciate that," Maria answered. "Not a lot of women in college have this experience, and my mother and I...are not close. I haven't really felt comfortable asking anyone before."

"Sometimes it's easier to ask a stranger."

Maria smiled sheepishly. "It is."

"But we all need a support network to help us through life's big changes. Do you have any family other than a sister you feel close to?"

Maria drew her shoulders forward and crossed her arms, looking down in thought. When she looked back up, the look she saw on the older woman's face was anything but judgmental. Instead, it encouraged her to open up. Taking a deep breath, Maria summed up her life. "Our parents had addiction issues our whole lives. Our dad died of an overdose when I was four, and our mother..." She trailed off, trying to think of a respectful way to explain their relationship.

"...is not motivated to seek recovery?" Kate said softly.

"Exactly. That's a really good way to say it." Encouraged by Kate's understanding and calm demeanor, Maria continued. "My sister and I were raised by an aunt on our dad's side, who was very kind to us. We lost her two years ago to a car accident."

"Wow, you've been through such a great deal."

Maria dropped her hands into her lap. "We have, but we've always had each other. It will be hard to live so far from Kayla, but Ansel promised to fly her up here twice a year for a visit."

Kate thought about how difficult it must be for a young woman to bring a baby into a world that has given her so much heartache; how unprepared and alone she must be feeling. Wanting to lift her spirits, Kate turned to more positive thoughts. "How did you and Ansel meet?"

"My roommate and his were dating, so we ended up in the same circles. The roommates broke up, but by then we were best friends. Over time, it transitioned so smoothly into dating that we really never had an official first date."

Kate smiled. "And how long have you been married?"

"About two years now. How about you?"

"Thirty-nine."

"That's a pretty good record. Any advice to help us get there?"

Kate's face fell as her eyes caught hold of a man moving toward them. Mud covered the left half of his suit, and by the way he was walking and muttering to himself, he was clearly not happy. She stood up, pushing up the sleeves of her sweatshirt.

Maria, still facing the water, sensed something was wrong. She turned her head as Kate stepped past her to see Ansel coming toward them, and immediately got out of the chair.

As he approached earshot, Maria asked, "Are you ok?"

Kate looked back at Maria, then at Ansel. Her brow furrowed as he answered.

"No. I'm sorry, but we need to go. Pack up your things."

"What happened?"

Ansel stepped around Kate with a loud sigh. "I don't have time to explain, just pack your stuff up and come with me." His voice gave increasing evidence of his lack of patience. "I'd help you, but as you can see, I. AM COVERED. IN. MUD!"

Maria quickly gathered her things into her little wagon, a confused look on her face. "I'm so sorry, Kate. I'll see you tomorrow, perhaps?"

"You have my number if you need it," Kate stressed.

Ansel took a deep breath, then addressed Maria more calmly. "I'm sorry, Maria, I've just had a horrible afternoon. I'll pull the wagon."

She handed him the wagon handle as he turned to Kate. "You don't know me, but I really am a nicer person than this. My name is Ansel. I'm Maria's husband. I'd shake your hand, but...". He raised his free hand, full of mud, to show the predicament.

Kate held out her hand to shake his, despite the issue. "Kate, nice to meet you. Your wife has been keeping me company this afternoon. I certainly hope you don't mind if I check in on her while you're here — considering her condition." Her gaze and the grip of her hand indicated more of a demand than a request.

"I'm-I'm sure she would appreciate that," he stammered. "I do apologize, but we really must be going."

Kate watched as the couple headed back to the cabin. Ansel and the wagon moved at a pace reflecting his stress level, while Maria followed about ten steps behind. Kate strained to hear what they were saying.

"Ansel, wait! I can't walk that fast," said Maria.

Ansel stopped walking. He turned back toward his wife, closed his eyes, and took a deep breath. "I'm sorry," Kate heard him say. When Maria caught up to him, he mumbled something more and started walking again. This time he walked slower, but still faster than she was able to keep up.

As Kate watched, they entered the cabin just across from her own. She decided her time at the water was done, and quickly made her way back inside. She shut the door behind her and opened the window over the sink. From there she could see their cabin.

With her hands shaking, Kate texted her husband. "Please come home. I'm ok, but I really need you here, and I can't explain right now. Please..."

She stared at the phone, praying he wasn't too far out on the water to get her text. Her prayers seemed answered when she received his nearly instant reply. "We're on our way."

For the next thirty minutes, Kate vacillated between pacing and pretending to wash dishes as she listened, watched and worried. The angle of the sun allowed her to remain in the shadows, unnoticed by anyone outside her cabin. She felt safe physically, but her concern for Maria connected her with what was happening next door.

While standing at the sink, movement in the young couple's cabin caught her eye. For a brief moment, Kate watched as Maria open the bedroom window. Before she could make out the expression on the young woman's face, however, Maria disappeared again behind the curtains. Kate rolled her right shoulder, which ached more than usual. *Everyone gets upset,* she told herself, *not everyone reacts the same.* Nevertheless, she glanced at the cabin door, assuring herself it was locked.

Did she hear talking? Kate froze at the sink, straining to make out if the sounds she was hearing were words. If so, what was being said? The color drained from her face as she realized she was hearing sobs and not words. Each sound confirmed her fears. Nearly collapsing into a nearby chair, she leaned over the table, weeping as past and present collided. It had been a long time since she felt this helpless.

The sound of the cabin's keypad unlocking the door made her stiffen, bringing her back to the present. She wiped her eyes as Angus walked in and closed the door.

"What's happened?" he asked.

"I don't know," she cried. "I'm not sure if I saw what I think I saw, but if I did..."

He pulled up a chair and sat next to her so she could cry on his shoulder. As she fit her face into the crevice, he put his arms around her, giving her the sense of safety she so desperately sought.

"Was it the couple in the next cabin?"

"How-how did you know?" She pulled back to see his face. "Did you see something?"

"On my way in, I saw them get in their car."

Kate jumped up and looked out the kitchen window, confused on how she missed seeing them. "I never heard them leave."

"She's clearly pregnant, and as I saw them, he looked a little . . . overly attentive and anxious. She seemed pretty worn out. I wouldn't have even noticed them really, but your text had me looking for anything odd as I came back. It seemed a likely trigger." He paused, waiting for her to face him again. "I want you to know — he didn't look angry when I saw them, so let's hope for the best for now, ok? Let me get you some water and you can tell me what you saw, and then we can talk about what to do, ok?"

Kate nodded and moved to a spot at the end of the sofa, while he grabbed them each some water from the refrigerator. She slowly related how she met Maria, their conversation about Ansel taking the young woman from her only close relative, and how putting his career first was leaving the young woman in a vulnerable state with no support. She then went into detail about his abruptness and the mud on his suit. "He wouldn't explain anything to her, he just demanded they go back to the cabin. I came back here and left the window open, just in case I needed to call the police. After a while, I heard her crying, and I just couldn't..." She took a gasp of air and looked at the pillow she held in her lap while she tried to slow her breathing again.

"You did the right thing," Angus assured, putting his arm around her and encouraging her to take a drink of water. "If you could hear her crying, you'd have heard if they were yelling at each other. You not hearing anything else was probably a good sign that things didn't get as bad as they could have."

Kate took a jagged breath, still trying to slow her breathing. "That's true," she said hopefully. "Maybe it was just an argument."

"Yeah, I'm not dismissing it fully, though. We have no proof one way or the other, but we can work with the odds until we know more."

"Gus, can we leave the front door open now that you're here? I just want to know when they get back that she's really ok. I want to see her for myself."

"Sure," he said, smiling. "It's kinda flattering to know you still think I can protect you, even with two fake knees."

"It's your cool head I depend on, and that's working just fine," she replied as he opened the door.

"You were supposed to let me know if you needed me," said Hank as he stepped onto the porch. "I just didn't want to leave until I knew for sure."

Angus wondered how he missed seeing his brother approach. "Sorry about that, I got caught up with what was going on. She'll be ok."

"Come on in, Hank," Kate called from the sofa, "We're on a stakeout."

"Well, if there's trouble, you won't be safe with this old man," he teased, pointing at his younger brother. "Can you even do a jumping jack anymore?"

"Right," agreed Angus, "What she needs are two old men. You whack him with a cane, and I'll tell him to get off our lawn. That'll show him."

Kate laughed, her nervous system appreciating the break from the strain.

"We're not that old," Hank muttered.

"We can barely get your boat in and out of the water ourselves anymore. Seriously, can you do a full jumping jack?" Angus asked.

"Where would I be without you guys?" Kate smiled appreciatively for the family she married into.

"Probably on a red carpet somewhere, surrounded by your fans," Hank said.

"Nah, she'd probably be on a beach flirting with some cabana boy," Angus teased.

"No cabana boy has anything on you," she told her husband, fluttering her eyelashes for effect.

"Seriously, though, what's going on?" Hank asked.

While Angus gave him the lowdown, Kate's despair turned to a more hopeful outcome. She decided to wear off the remaining adrenaline by throwing together some dinner for the three of them. While her ears stayed on alert, she allowed her heart the pause of enjoying their company.

Games of gin rummy and cribbage were fought and won while cars came and went from the resort's parking lot. As each car door opened and closed, the three took turns getting up to watch for the couple in question.

Somewhere around eleven o'clock, they pulled in. Angus turned off the cabin light as he quietly spoke. "I think this is them. It's the same car, but they're both dressed differently than they were before."

Kate and Hank rushed to the screen door to look. They watched quietly as Ansel got out and ran around to help Maria out of the car.

"Oh, she is definitely pregnant," said Hank.

"Shh...they'll hear you," said Angus.

Kate, tired of trying to see around the taller men, moved over to the window at the sink. She watched as Ansel and Maria slipped inside, laughing. Through the cracks in the curtains, the three could discern only the movement of the couple from the main room to the bedroom, and then into darkness.

"I hope I've overreacted," said Kate wistfully.

"Maybe we should take him fishing tomorrow, just to be sure," said Angus.

"And if he's innocent, we'll bring him back," said Hank.

Kate looked at Hank seriously. "How would you know for sure?"

"You know we're not ones for vigilante justice," said Angus. "Hank's just teasing. For tonight, at least, it seems she's ok. Maybe we should all get some sleep." He then turned to Hank. "You ok getting the boat back home?"

"Barely an inconvenience. I'll just leave the boat connected and park it on the street." Hank opened the door to leave. How about I pick up something for breakfast tomorrow?"

"I'll make the coffee," said Angus.

The next morning, Kate caught a whiff of coffee and despite tossing and turning most of the night, decided to start her day.

As she entered the kitchen, Angus handed her a cup. She gratefully took a sip and set it on the table while she put on her shoes.

"How'd you sleep?" he asked.

"I don't even know," she said. "I feel like a truck hit me, but I'm hoping to figure out a way to talk to Maria this morning.   If nothing else, she'll know she has someone to turn to. How did you sleep?"

"Not so great, either. Around six this morning, I went to sit on the porch. Saw — what's his name next door — he was leaving. A little later, he came back with flowers. Seemed a little guilty looking. Noticed a donut tire on the front of the car, too. Looks like he really needs that job. Not sure what to think of it all yet."

As he said that, the sound of a car door opening and closing came through the still open kitchen window. They looked at each other, then went to the window to watch Ansel back out of his parking spot and drive away.

"You think he's leaving her?" Angus asked.

"I don't know, I can't tell what's what."

A knock at the door startled them both. "It's probably her," said Kate. She held her breath as Angus opened the door.

"I brought some Breakfast Pasties, fresh from Miners. They're still warm," Hank said as he stepped inside. "I wasn't sure what would be going on here, so I brought a few extra. Figured you could always save some for tomorrow."

Kate had no idea how hungry she was until she smelled them. "You are amazing! Thank you so much."

"Good pick, Sir," Angus said as Hank set them on the table.

"Almost had to eat one on the way here, the truck smelled so good."

Kate, already putting together a tray, made clear her idea. "Hey, would you guys be offended if I took one over to Maria? Even if I wake her up, this would be a good excuse to check on her."

The guys both nodded their approval. "You feel like eating ours on the porch, Hank?" Angus asked. "Maybe we could make sure you ladies have enough time to talk."

Kate crossed the path with a cutting board carrying two cups of coffee and two breakfast pasties. The breakfast platter was protected from insects by a thin towel. Summoning her past waitressing skills, she balanced the board on one hand over her shoulder and knocked on the door.

After a long pause, the door opened. Maria squinted into the sun, trying to see without her contacts. "Hello?"

"Good morning," said Kate, bringing the makeshift serving tray back down from her shoulder. "I hope you don't mind, but I noticed Ansel was gone, and I thought I'd bring you some breakfast."

Maria's face lit up as she looked at the tray Kate uncovered to show her. "It smells wonderful, thank you so much. Come on in. I'm afraid I'm not quite awake yet. I don't even have my contacts in." She raked her hands through her hair and said, "I must look a mess."

"You look beautiful!" said Kate. "I just wanted to check in and see how you are. You go ahead and finish getting dressed, and I will put these things on the table."

"Ok...ah, thank you! This is so nice of you, really," she said as she walked into the bathroom.

Kate raised her voice slightly, so as to be heard from the other room. "Well, I've been pregnant, and I know how it is. You'll be making plenty of breakfasts to come. My brother-in-law picked up these pasties for us this morning, and we had an extra one."

Maria poked out her head, pausing in the middle of tying a ponytail. "What's a pasty?"

"Oh, are you in for a treat! It's a meat pie you hold in your hands. He got them from a place called Miners Pasty Kitchen over in Munising, where he lives. Everybody just calls them 'Miners'."

Maria came into the kitchen, now dressed and refreshed, able to see clearly the pasties in question. She looked at the kitchen chair across from Kate and picked up the coffee. After taking a sip, she said, "Do you mind if we sit in the living room? I just can't with these chairs this morning."

"Not a problem," said Kate, putting the pasties back on the board.

As they moved to the sofa, Kate gave a short synopsis of the history of the Pasty and their connection with the local miners.

Maria took her first bite, then breathed in and out while covering her mouth.

"Still hot?" Kate asked.

She nodded as she chewed and swallowed. "Oh, I could get used to these," she said. "They're amazing! How are they still so warm?"

"Cornish secret, I assume," answered Kate, shrugging. "I don't make them, I just eat them whenever we come...Hey, how did Ansel's interview go? Did he find out anything?"

Maria face could barely hold her smile as she answered. "He did! In fact, we had to leave so quickly yesterday because we were invited to a fundraising event for the school. He starts in three weeks, which gives us just enough time to find a place to live before he leaves to go back and finish moving us."

"I'm so glad to hear that. Sounds like you have a lot of work to do, and quickly."

Maria's phone buzzed with a message from Ansel, letting her know he would be back soon to pick her up.

"How long before he gets here?"

"About half an hour," Maria answered, sipping her coffee.

"Look, there's something I want to talk to you about. I know I've only known you for a day, and I don't mean to be putting my nose where it doesn't belong, but I want to make sure you're ok."

"In what way?" Maria asked, a look of puzzlement emphasizing the question.

Kate looked away for a moment, then started to fidget. "There are . . . certain situations that women can find themselves in that they never thought they would. Situations that are isolating — hard to get out of."

"Are you talking about yesterday?"

"Well, your husband was quite upset, and I just want to make sure . . . well, um . . ." Kate took a breath and let it out. "I heard you crying last night, and I've known situations where . . . This morning, my husband was sitting on the porch having coffee and saw Ansel bring you flowers, which fits a kind of a pattern of . . . well . . . we just want you to know we're here for you if you need help."

Maria sat dumfounded for a moment. She opened her mouth to speak, then closed it again.

Kate's nervousness increased, causing her to keep explaining. "It's not just that, but here you are, moving away from your family into a place where you know no one, in order for him to advance his career. None of these alone are a problem, but altogether, it creates — a cause for concern." Having said all she could say, Kate sighed and braced herself for the defensive reaction she knew was in store.

"I–I can't tell you how much it means to me that you would put yourself out there like that for me." She paused, then admitted, "I'm not so naive that I don't know you risked a great deal to talk to me about this."

Kate's shoulders dropped, for the first time hopeful for a misunderstanding. "So, you're saying I'm wrong?"

"Yes!" Maria said as she laughed nervously. She then put down her pasty, leaned forward and locked eyes with Kate. "I want you to know Ansel has never put a hand on me in that way. As far as the isolation, that's for my benefit. I mean, I want my sister here, but I'm not asking her to move for us ."

"Please forgive me for being a nosy old woman." Kate placed her empty plate back on the cutting board, becoming nervous once again.

"There's nothing to forgive here. In fact, I couldn't be more grateful. Most people would have just let things happen and close their eyes. My childhood was full of that. Do you mind if I tell you more of our story?"

"It would really set my mind at ease, but you don't have to."

"I want to." Maria turned sideways on the sofa to face Kate fully. "Ansel was an Assistant Professor at UCLA when we found out I was pregnant. Being a sociologist, he is very aware of the career setbacks many women experience when raising a family, and it bothers him. In fact, it bothered him so much that he insisted we move here so he could take a similar job at a less prestigious university."

"But what does one have to do with the other? I don't understand, how does that help your career?"

Maria smiled. "Well, I'm afraid I made the mistake early on of telling him my career goals. Now he's determined to make sure I reach them. I'm a Marine Biologist, and I would love to work on the Great Lakes. He made sure we moved here so I could do just that once the kids are in school. We decided to move before our first child is born so that horrible cross-country ride didn't have to be endured in a car seat. It just took us this long to figure out how to make it all happen. As you said, sometimes nine months is not enough."

Kate laughed at the irony of those words being used in such a positive way. "I'm sorry," she said, dabbing a napkin to her eyes, "I'm just so relieved. You have no idea how worried I was."

Maria put her hand on Kate's arm. "Kate, have you had to live through something that would cause you to have this kind of reaction?"

Kate nodded. "My pregnancy, along with the help of some friends, gave me the courage to leave him. It's why my eldest slept in a box for a while. I just had so little monetarily."

"I'm so sorry, Kate!"

"Well, it's all water under the bridge now . . . or so I thought, until yesterday. I guess I still have some healing to do. Knowing your husband is good to you is very helpful for that." Kate smiled as she took a deep breath and let it out slowly.

"Oh, I almost forgot! Would you like to see the flowers? They're very pretty." Maria went to the bedroom and came out with a beautiful bouquet of roses in a crystal vase.

"Oh, those are beautiful," Kate said. "He has very good taste."

"Thank you." Maria placed them in the middle of the kitchen table. "I should explain what happened yesterday. It is all so funny now."

"Would you mind terribly if I just quick run back to our cabin real quick and let the guys know everything's ok? They're on the porch, just in case I needed backup".

"How about I go with you so they can see for themselves that I'm ok? We should probably get them caught up before Ansel gets back."

While Maria slipped on her shoes, Kate gathered the cups, plates and cutting board to bring them back with them. As she did, she thought about the wonderful opportunities available to Maria. Suddenly, their previous conversation made more sense. "That's why you knew so much about the Lake Trout!"

"Old as the dinosaurs," Maria said, winking.

"Wow, you're a smart girl!"

"Lot of smart girls paved the way for me. Ready?" she asked as she held the door open.

Angus and Hank stopped talking as they approached. After inviting Maria in for a comfortable spot to sit, Kate introduced her to the men, stressing her role as a Marine Biologist.

"She knows where all the fish are!" said Hank.

"Yeah, well, she's not dumb enough to tell us," Angus said to Hank. He then turned toward Maria. "If you want to keep fish in the lakes, do not tell this man where they are. I'm pretty sure you're sworn to secrecy, right? Some sort of government clearance?"

"Of course," Maria said, "it's a matter of national security."

"I knew it!" said Hank. "That's why we couldn't find 'em yesterday. Ever since she came into town, they've been gone."

Kate laughed. "So, I never found out, what happened that Ansel was so full of mud yesterday?"

"Here's the dumb part – I don't really know. Here's what happened. We went back into the cabin after that embarrassing conversation at the beach, and he explained that he got the job. He also explained that we had two hours to get to a fundraiser the dean was throwing. I didn't bring dress clothes, and he only had the one suit. He jumped in the shower and I started scraping the mud from his shoes to see if we could save the expense of buying another pair, and I guess the relief of knowing he had the job he wanted overcame me. The sobbing you heard last night was from relief. I had no idea how much tension I was carrying around until that moment. Thankfully, I had time to cry it out a little before having to be around a bunch of strangers. After I had the chance to rinse off and do something with my hair, we had to hurry to shop for a suit and an appropriate dress for me."

Maria paused for a moment, holding her belly. "The baby's kicking, sorry." She adjusted accordingly. "Apparently, he thinks this is funny, too ... Anyway, we get in the car, and I asked Ansel, 'Why do I feel lopsided?'.

Turns out the front tire on my side was a spare tire. He pulls onto the highway right over here with a top speed of 45. I have to say, people in Michigan are a lot nicer about having to go around than they were where we're from. Anyway, when he told me the event had valet parking, I made him pull into a gas station because I was laughing so hard, I nearly peed my p ants!"

"Oh, that is funny!" said Kate.

"It took most of the time getting there for him to tell me all about the interview and the campus, and I guess we just forgot the part about the mud. I assumed he fell while changing the tire." Maria started laughing so hard she could barely finish the story. "Can you imagine us driving up to the valet parking with a donut tire and garbage bags over the driver's seat? He'd put one on it because of the mud from his suit. You should've seen the looks on their faces! Thankfully, the party was at the back of the building, so the valets were the only ones that saw us. Once we were inside, his new colleagues and their spouses took enough interest in getting to know us individually that we barely got to talk to each other. I even found some research projects I might be able to help with while at home with the kids. Mostly computer work, of course, but an hour here and there in the evenings can keep my skills sharp. By the time we came back here, I was so physically, emotionally and socially exhausted, I pretty much just fell over and zonked out."

"I can't believe how different that is from what it looked like." Kate said.

Angus clapped his hands together. "Well, if you and Ansel are up to it, Hank and I would like to take you all out for dinner. There's a lot here to celebrate."

Hank looked at Angus. "We do? Oh, yes, we do." He winked at Maria to let her know he was teasing.

Since the day they first met, Kate had been placing one unsalted in-shell peanut at the base of the squirrel's tree every day. Today, he was waiting for her in the distance, unnoticed. She pulled two peanuts out of her pocket and put them at the base of the tree and backed up. "Good-bye, little guy," she whispered to the tree tops.

As she walked away, she looked back just in time to see him grab the peanuts. She stopped to watch. He shoved one in his mouth, then the other, and disappeared up the back of the tree once again. She wondered briefly, as she looked up at the branches, how many generations of squirrels had come and gone since she was a girl?

Back at the cabin, she picked up the guestbook and flipped to a blank spot. Her arthritic hands struggled to write as elegantly as in times past, especially considering the small lines. When finished, she reviewed the results. Satisfied at its legibility, she closed the book and set down the pen. □

Name: Angus and Kate
From: Marshfield
Highlight: The deep blue horizon

A Fine Education

J asper looked at his great grandson with concern. "Don't you have to be at least five feet tall to go out on Gitche Gumee? I'm pretty sure there's a law about that."

Connor's countenance dropped. "I'm four feet, eleven inches...is that close enough?".

"Well," said Jasper, slowly losing the ability to keep a straight face, "they passed that law 'cause the fish can eat you in one bite if you're shorter than five feet."

"I'm at least two bites!"

"Alright, then, we'll have to bring a baseball bat just in case the fish mistake you for the bait. You see what your Oma might have for us to bring for snacks, and I'll go get my shoes."

Moments later, Jasper and Connor exited the cabin completely outfitted for fishing, including a plastic pail of cookies baked by Oma Winnie.

"Do you know why you catch more fish on the big lake than on the other great lakes?" Jasper asked.

"Why?"

"Because it's Superior!"

Connor rolled his eyes and groaned, but could not hold back a chuckle as he climbed into the waiting car. Opa Jasper was his favorite person, and days fishing with him were his favorite.

That was, until today.

A mere hour and a half after launching the boat, the four generations of Jenssen men returned.

Connor's mom, grandma and Opa Winnie were getting ready to leave for Marquette when the men pulled in. "What's happened?" Winnie asked.

"No big thing, Connor just had a little fish feeding incident. We were thinking of letting him rest up a bit and then fishing from shore if he's up for it," said Jasper.

As Connor's mother went to check on him, Jasper continued. "He's already got some color back. A few saltines, a little nap, and he'll be ready to catch some sharks soon."

"The great lakes don't have sharks," Connor said quietly, his hand still on his queasy stomach as he slowly got out of the car.

"They did before I came fishing here," replied Jasper. "Hey, how about you and I go watch tv in my cabin and your dad and grandpa can take care of the boat? I'll even let you pick what we watch." Turning to his son and grandson, he said, "If you guys want to go back out, I can stay here with him. My stomach was rolling a little, too, so maybe it's best if he and I both fish from shore."

Connor's parents, Mark and Chelsea, glanced at each other, each wanting the other to decide.

"You people just go do your thing. Connor and I are going to talk about how I fished all those sharks out of the great lakes." said Jasper.

"You ok with that, Connor?" his dad asked.

For Connor, his great-grandfather was always an adventure. He suspected some of Opa Jasper's stories were made up, but they sparked his imagination. Opa Jasper was always full of puns and jokes, which were especially appreciated by the young man who took himself too seriously. His face lit up a little as he nodded, which was all the confirmation Chelsea needed.

Mark agreed. "Grandpa's got a phone, and Connor has a smart watch. They can call if there's a problem, right?"

Connor held up his newly obtained smart watch proudly, as Jasper nodded.

"Then it's settled. Thank you so much, Grandpa! I will bring you back some of that famous carrot cake we read about," said Chelsea.

After a few moments of fussing over Connor, the two middle generation Jenssen men went back to fish the waters of Lake Superior, and the ladies went to find whatever treasures awaited them in the shops of Marquette.

An hour later, Jasper and Connor were having themselves a sandwich and some chips, discussing the major issues affecting modern man, like video game strategy, favorite teachers, and what to do if they encounter a bear.

"But what if Grandpa can run faster than you?" Connor asked.

"You didn't know that's why us old guys use canes, did you? People think we use them to help us walk, but really, we use them to trip people if a bear is after us." They both laughed as he mimicked thrusting his invisible cane before an imaginary victim.

Connor took a bite of his sandwich, thinking as he chewed. "Hey, Opa, how old do you think this cabin is? Do you think it's from pioneer days?"

Having arrived the evening before, Jasper barely noticed the accommodations for his vacation. Preoccupied with fishing, he hadn't really thought that much about the resort at all. Now, however, he scrutinized the cabin's details. "It's pretty old. In fact, I think it might be older than me."

"How long do you think it took to make it?"

"Oh, it likely took a while. This would have been made with pretty much a saw and an axe. Each of these logs is probably a whole tree wide, and then they would have had to cut each log into this square shape and stack them just so. It looks like it would have been simple, but there's a lot to it, and I imagine it was hard work. They did a pretty good job if it's still here, though."

"So where do they get the rocks for the fireplace?"

"They probably found them in the field they were planning to farm. The stones would have been in the way, so it kind of worked out that they needed a fireplace."

"So then why does that one stick out?"

Jasper turned to look at the fireplace. Not seeing any stick out further than the other, he contorted his face to see if that brought anything more into focus. "I don't see any sticking out. Which one are you talking about?"

"That one over there, on the side," Connor said before putting the last potato chip in his mouth.

"I still don't see it. Show me."

Connor walked to the right side of the fireplace and crouched down. He touched a stone close to the wall. "This one," he said as he looked at it closer. "It looks kinda weird."

Jasper's curiosity was peaked. "Let me see that." He groaned as he got up from the table and shuffled over to look. He cocked his head, wondering if there was something behind the stone. "I think you may have just found something."

Connor's eyes got wide. "Like a treasure?"

"Well, let's find out. See these small cracks in the mortar? That might mean something. Go get a butter knife from the drawer. We're going to need something slim to get between the rock and the mortar." Jasper put his hand on the stone and shook it, trying to figure out if it was loose. The mortar let loose slightly, allowing the stone to wobble. "How did you even see this? It hardly sticks out at all."

"I don't know," said Connor, "I could only see it while I was sitting down. I had to remember which one it was when I walked over."

"Well, you've got some good eyes there, kid. Must've gotten that from my side." Jasper tried to get the butter knife between the rock and the mortar, but the size of the end of the knife was working against him. Frustrated, Jasper asked Connor to go to his truck and get his hammer and a flathead screwdriver.

"Are we going to get in trouble?" Connor asked as he handed over the tools.

"I hadn't thought of that," said Jasper. "Well...whatever treasure we find, we'll share it with the people who own this place. Besides . . . we can probably find a hardware store and just replace the mortar. It'll be good as new, maybe better."

The first whack of the hammer to the back end of the screwdriver was louder than Connor expected, causing him to put his hands over his ears until the pounding stopped.

"Hey, would you look at that?" Jasper said, putting down the tools. The loose stone before him was now in two pieces.

The two of them stood staring at the situation, trying to figure out how they were going to cover up their discovery. After a moment's thought, Connor had an idea. "We could super glue it," he said.

"Good idea!"

It was a horrible idea, but Jasper didn't feel like explaining why. He used the screwdriver to pry the two pieces of stone out of their resting place and peered inside, blocking Connor's view.

"What's in there?"

Jasper reached his hand in the dark shadow of the hole behind the stones. Carefully, he pulled out a dark leather case wrapped in what was left of a piece of cloth.

"What is it?" Connor asked as Jasper unwrapped the cloth.

"I don't know, but it looks to be very, very old, so we're going to be extra careful with it." The case had a small buckle holding it closed, which Jasper delicately opened. He then looked from what was in his hands to the 10-year-old face full of wonder in front of him. "Should we open it?" He asked.

Connor nodded enthusiastically.

Jasper slowly opened the lid, being careful to not put pressure on the hinge. "Woah," he whispered.

"What are they? Binoculars?"

"Kind of. They're called opera glasses." Seeing the confused look on Connor's face, he elaborated. "If you were sitting in a theater or opera house, you could use these to see the faces of the performers. They didn't have big TV screens so you could see what's going on."

"Cool, can I see them?"

"How about you sit down, and I'll let you look at them on your lap? This isn't something even I am comfortable holding too long. They're probably worth quite a bit."

Connor sat on the sofa and tried to look through the glasses.

"There's a dial you can use to focus the glasses. That is, if it still works. Be careful, though, if it doesn't move easily. Don't force it."

"How do you keep them on your face?"

"You don't, you have to hold them up. Some used to have handles to make it easier. Do you see a flashlight anywhere? I want to see if there's anything else in there, but it's too dark."

"There's one on your phone. If it works like my mom's, you can just chop with it and it turns on and off."

"Chop with it?"

"Yeah, let me show you." Connor carefully set the opera glasses on the sofa and grabbed the phone from the table. He then turned it sideways and shook it, mimicking chopping wood. The light responded, making the young man quite pleased. He then handed the phone to his great-grandfather.

"Well, I'll be . . . I didn't know you could do that!" Jasper mimicked what he saw, and the light turned off. He did it again and the light went on.

"Genius! Ok, let's see if there's anything else . . . What's this?" he asked, pulling out an envelope.

His phone buzzed in his hand, then started ringing. Jasper startled, dropping the envelope to the ground. As Connor raced to grab it, Jasper exclaimed, "Don't open it yet! Hold on."

Jasper looked at the phone and saw it was Winnie. He knew he had to answer.

"Hello?"

"Hello. How are things going?" Winnie asked.

"We're fine. He's feeling better."

"Ok, good. We're planning to come back after we stop for some gas and a couple of groceries. I was wondering if there was anything you or Connor would like me to pick up?"

"Uh...we're good, thanks. See you soon." Jasper went to set the phone down, but the flashlight glared in his eyes. He again double-chopped the phone and the light went off. "That is the neatest thing," he mumbled, still in awe of the technology. "Now, let's have a look at what's in the envelope, shall we?"

They sat at the table, eager to learn what was inside the secret envelope. Jasper held his breath while he opened the flap. Whatever glue was there before was long gone.

It felt like forever to Connor as he watched his great-grandfather cautiously slide the folded paper out onto the table and unfold it. "What does it say?"

Jasper skimmed the letter, then read it aloud.

June 25, 1905

Dear Mrs. Nicolls,

I would like to congratulate you and Mr. Nicolls on your recent nuptials.

You have been an outstanding teacher these many years, and a favorite of my children. Many a day they have returned home and told me of your enthusiasm for not only the required subject matter, but for culture and the arts as well. Your reputation with the community is one of which to be proud.

As a token of my appreciation for your contributions to the enlightenment of our youth, I am sending two tickets to an upcoming operetta, entitled, 'Miss D.Q. Pons'. It will be showing at the Marquette Opera House on July the third. This operetta was written by a dear friend of the family, a Mr. Will Adams and a Miss Norma Ross.

In order to assure your enjoyment of the evening, I have also included a pair of opera glasses, which I purchased on our trip to Paris especially for this occasion.

Please enjoy the evening, and know that your hard work in instilling our city's youth with knowledge and culture will live on for generations.

Sincerely,

Mrs. J. Eddy

Jasper was the first to express his thoughts. "Wow, that was quite a gift! No wonder they kept it hidden."

"Yeah," said Connor, "she must have been a good teacher."

"Hey, you feeling up to going into town with me? I'm pretty sure they have a little museum somewhere. Maybe we could find out more about her. Maybe she has some great-great grandkids that should get these."

"Should we wait for Mom and Dad to come back first?"

"Nah, we can sweep up the mess and just go. If the rest of the family sees these, they'll form a committee and push us out. We won't even get a chance to solve the mystery ourselves. In fact," he added with a gleam in his eye, "we should hurry up and leave before they get here."

Jasper grabbed his hat and opened the door. As they got into the car, he asked Connor to send his mother a text to let her know they were running to town for a bit.

Chelsea read the message out loud and sent her agreement as the cars passed each other coming and going.

The ladies hadn't noticed the grey van, but Jasper definitely saw them. "We got out just in time," he said. Congratulating himself on keeping the adventure between the bookend generations of the family, Jasper offered a high-five to his more-than-willing accomplice. "Here," he said, handing Connor his phone, "You're the navigator. Look up where the museum is. When you find it, tell me how to get there."

Due to Connor's navigational success, the two soon found themselves walking into the Marquette Regional History Center, carrying their treasures. "Now, we're not going to tell people where we found these, you hear?"

Connor nodded, deciding it was best if he stayed quiet.

"Good afternoon, gentlemen, how are you today?" asked the receptionist, pushing his glasses back in place.

"We'd be better if you could help us learn more about these antiques," said Jasper. "We're not from here, so we really don't know the history associated with them."

"Without asking you to open the letter, can you tell me what it says? It's good to not handle the paper too much if it's as old as it looks."

"It's explaining the opera glasses are a gift to a teacher from around here."

"Well, Mr. —"

"My name's Jasper, and this is my great-grandson, Connor."

"Nice to meet you. Please, have a seat. Normally, we operate only by appointment for this kind of thing, but I'll see if our Research Librarian is available. I think she'd like to see these."

As Jasper and Connor took a seat on a padded bench in the lobby, Connor's watch rang. "What do I tell Mom?"

"Just say 'Hello', I'll answer her questions."

"Hello, Mom!"

"Connor, is everything ok? Where are you?"

"Hello Chelsea, we're fine," Jasper said. "There was an issue with the fireplace, and I figured I'd teach Connor how to fix it. We're in town getting mortar. He's feeling much better, so I was wondering if I could I bring him to get some ice cream before we head back?" The old man smiled at the boy knowingly, adding a wink as he watched Connor's face light up and nod.

"I'm sure he would love that, Opa."

Jasper agreed to be back well before supper, and they hung up. Turning to Connor, he explained, "I figured asking about ice cream would buy us some time, just in case."

In unison, they turned toward the sound of the approaching footsteps. "Hello, my name is Beth. I understand you have some interesting items you'd like some information about?"

"We do and we would, Beth." answered Jasper.

"Would you mind, please, following me upstairs? We can take the elevator."

At one of the tables in the Research Library, Beth carefully laid out the glasses and the letter.

"What a beautiful pair of opera glasses. This looks like brass and mother-of-pearl." She read the name on the eyepieces, "LeMaire FI, Paris". Using a magnifying glass, she looked closer at the icons engraved alongside the name. "Oh, those are bees. You know, these are beautifully made. I'm not an antiques dealer, but these may have some value. You may wish to have them appraised. When you add the letter to it, I'll bet they tell quite a story. Let's see what it has to say, shall we?"

After reading the letter aloud, she looked up at the two men. "These are fascinating. How did you come across them?"

Connor looked to Jasper, who became uncomfortable in his chair and shifted accordingly. "We found them."

Beth waited for more explanation, but got none.

Jasper moved the conversation along in a direction more comfortable to him. "So how would a person go about researching this kind of thing?"

"That is a good question. For something like this, we'd be looking for school records, obituaries, marriage records, and descendants. We likely could find a newspaper article for the opera she attended as well. The opera house always took out an advertisement in the paper for their performances, so that should be easier to find. I imagine there is a lot of history connected to this teacher, but it may not be quite as documented as the opera. You never know, though, we are sometimes surprised ourselves by what we can dig up."

"How long would it take to find all that out?" Connor asked.

"We're only here until Sunday, and we'd like to find the descendants, if possible," said Jasper.

"Let me see what I can find in that time. Would you mind filling out this form? It gives me the information I need to start from, as well as your written permission to move forward in the research."

"How's your handwriting, kid?" Jasper asked. "Mine's a bit shaky. You fill it out, and I'll sign it, how's that?"

Connor nodded in agreement, picking up the pen.

"I hope you gentlemen don't mind, but I have an appointment coming at any moment. Once you're done filling it out, please give it to the lady at the desk behind you, and I'll get started on the research today. It was a pleasure to meet you both. Thank you for letting us be a part of your journey with this." She stood up to leave and shook their hands.

"We look forward to hearing from you, Beth. Thank you, and thank you for seeing us unannounced." Jasper's firm handshake confirmed his satisfaction with their meeting.

Back at the car, Connor was again in charge of navigating. The promise of ice cream not forgotten, he quickly found Jilbert Dairy on the internet. "Cool! Opa, this one has a giant cow! Can we go there?"

Jasper chuckled. "If you can tell me how to get there, we can."

They soon found themselves sitting at a picnic table in the shade of Jilly, the giant cow statue.

"We're going to need to get some super glue on the way back," said Connor before licking a drip of ice cream from his sugar cone.

"Yeah, about that... I was thinking maybe mortar would be a better idea. Let me explain why, and you decide what you think we should do."

Connor listened as Jasper explained what he knew of masonry, and how super glue generally isn't made for a porous surface, such as sandstone. The two-man committee decided mortar would be better, and agreed to pick some up on the way back.

At the cabin, Connor opened the door for Jasper, who was now exhausted from the day's events. He surveyed the faces as he entered. "What's for dinner? It smells like someone caught some fish!"

The two younger women looked at Winnie. "Where's the mortar?" she asked.

"What mortar?"

"The mortar to fix the fireplace?" asked Mark.

"Oh...yeah," said Jasper. "I guess we forgot it."

"Jasper, what is going on?" Winnie asked.

Turning to his partner in all of this, he said, "Well, Kid, I guess we have to come clean."

Having contained himself the better part of the day, Connor could hold it in no longer. "We found a hidden treasure!"

Chelsea was skeptical. "Why don't you tell us all about it while we eat?"

Jasper let Connor do the talking, interjecting details here and there. The family discussed what they knew of the history of the area, but no one knew of a Mrs. Nicolls.

Hours later, Jasper and Winnie sat on the sofa next to one another.

"You know, for right or for wrong, what you found belongs to the owner of the cabin. It would have been sold with the cabin, and no longer the property of the family. You might be in trouble just for disturbing it."

"Well, that's just dumb, it belongs to the family."

"It should, but you may want to talk to the owner before someone finds out where you got it. They could report it as stolen property."

Jasper thought it over. "I don't like that you're right, but you are. I don't want to make an elephant out of a mouse."

"You're a good man, Mr. Jenssen," she said softly as she put her head on his shoulder.

He put his arm around her shoulder. "And you're a good woman, Mrs. Jenssen."

The next morning, true to his word, Jasper went to see Kristofer and Ingrid while the rest of the family waited in the cabin. He introduced himself, explained what was found, and handed them the items.

"You know," Jasper said, "in a town this rich in history, it would be a shame if someone who had such an impact was forgotten by time. My great-grandson and I took it over to the museum so they could tell us what the history was. They're checking to see if they can find any descendants of the teacher around, as well."

Kristofer looked at his wife, who was busy rereading the letter. "Can you show us where you found these in the fireplace?" he asked.

"Sure. Just so you know, though, I had some experience in my youth with masonry. I may not be able to carve a statue, but this is something I can fix before I leave."

Ingrid and Kristofer followed Jasper to the cabin, where they inspected the hole, as well as the broken stone.

Ingrid looked from the empty opening to the letter and leather case in her hand, then to Kristofer. "To think, this would have been lost if..."

Kristofer nodded, then changed the subject. "The couple must have a number of descendants by now, and the last thing we need is some sort of legal family fight. We will have to find a way to contact them."

"I wonder if she would have taught any of our grandparents?" Ingrid asked.

"Now, that would be remarkable," said Jasper.

"Maybe the museum could have it and let everyone share it," said Connor.

The room full of adults looked to the young man in astonishment, then to Kristofer and Ingrid.

"That sounds like a fine idea, if the family also agrees to donate it. What do you think, Kristofer?"

"I'd be happy to see it go where it can be properly preserved."

Jasper smiled. "Then I'll get a hold of Beth at the museum and let her know you are the contacts for this, if that's ok?"

Ingrid and Kristofer nodded in agreement.

A few days later, Jasper and Connor painstakingly finished fixing the fireplace. They celebrated their handiwork by setting off to the shoreline, fishing poles in hand.

"What do you think we could use for bait if we're looking to catch a shark?" Jasper asked.

"I thought you said you fished them all out of the Great Lakes."

"Oh, that's right. I forgot. Maybe we could catch a giant squid then. You got any giant squid bait in your tackle box?"

"I'm not sure. What do they eat?"

Hearing footsteps coming quickly behind them, Connor stopped and turned to see Kristofer trying to catch up. "Jasper, Connor, we have news!"

Jasper stopped and turned as well. "Hello, Kristofer! Did the museum lady call?"

"Yes, Beth called and spoke to Ingrid, letting her know what she has found. Ingrid is contacting the descendants as we speak, to let them know of the find, and to see if they would have any arguments to us donating the items."

"That's great! What else did you find out?"

Kristofer's face went from excited to serious. "Beth is going to send us an email with some more details, but here's what we know. The teacher's maiden name was Catherine Maes. She came here from France with her grandparents as a child, and later became a teacher. When she was 23, she met a Mr. Frederick Nicolls, and they decided to marry. He bought this land and built this cabin, along with what was needed to run a farm. That's about when Mrs. Eddy decided to show her appreciation for all the hard work she'd done as a teacher. Unfortunately, Mrs. Nicholls died in childbirth in 1907."

"The letter was dated 1905, so they'd only been married about two years. How sad," said Jasper.

"The good news is that the baby lived. Apparently, Frederick grieved for a bit, then remarried so his son would have a mother. I forget her name, but it will be in the email. That couple went on to have more children. The son, whose name was Reynart, became a teacher himself and had a big family. The communities between here and Marquette are pretty strongly educated by the Nicholls family. Beth believes that perhaps the things you found had been sealed up for safekeeping, with the intention of one day giving them to their son. For whatever reason, they must have been forgotten in time."

"Until now," said Connor.

As the repair to the fireplace cured, four generations of Janssens loaded up their cars and said their good-byes'.

"I'm just going to take one more look around to make sure we didn't forget anything," Winnie said.

The guestbook sat on a small table to the side of the fireplace, catching her eye. She'd read some of the comments during the week, but had not addressed their own entry yet. She paged through the long line of guests that came before them, each oblivious to the hopeful newlyweds that first graced this cabin, and to the plight of a new father and son who had to make their way in the world without the woman they loved the most.

Both saddened by the legacy and proud of the determined spirit the original owners showed, Winnie felt very honored to have stayed in their home. Finding the next open spot, she added a line for Jasper and herself, adding Connor for good measure.□

Name: Jasper and Winnie and Connor

From: Marinette

Highlight: A fine education.

Fireflies

The waves of the shoreline were small, but the sound they made became deafening as her question sank in. He could barely get the words out. "I-I thought he was with you."

"You said you'd watch him!" Abbie's face showed her panic.

His mind raced to remember saying such a thing. Nope, couldn't find it. "When did I say that?"

"When you were talking to Gary!"

"I thought you asked if I was chillin'!"

"No, I asked if you'd watch Dylan! I had to get stuff from the cabin."

The water. Please, God, don't let him be in the water. "He had his life jacket on, right?"

"Yeah, we made sure, remember?"

"Has anyone seen Dylan?" He shouted to the crowd of family and friends that rented the resort for the weekend.

Heads turned. Other parents checked for their children, and then went about asking if the other kids saw him.

While Abbie and the rest of the family started checking the cabins and the woods, Marcus headed straight to the water, calling his son's name.

The water made no answer.

A half-hour later, the couple sat in the cabin, describing what their son was wearing that day. "Jeans, a blue t-shirt, his favorite shoes...they're red — helped him go fast," said Abbie.

"Being red, I'm sure they do," Michigan State Trooper Jacobsen said. "You mentioned he was wearing a life jacket?"

"Ah, yes. We were afraid of him running off into the water. The autism, you know. We weren't actually planning to go swimming today." Marcus answered.

"What color was it?"

"Bright orange, just your basic vest style."

While Marcus answered questions, Abbie second-guessed everything she remembered. Was his t-shirt blue, or had she put the green one on? No, she definitely remembered it matching his new hat. *His new hat!* In her hopefulness of remembering something new, she blurted out the details. "His Uncle Frank gave him a baseball cap when we first got here! A blue one, with a backhoe on it. Dylan was pretty excited."

Anything new she could think of felt like a step closer to finding him. For the last half hour, though, she vacillated between feelings of weakness, rage and anguish. For now, Dylan needed her to hold it together. She could give in to her feelings later. She took a deep breath, feeling the walls of the cabin start to close in.

Abbie may not have known where Dylan was, but she sure knew where he wasn't. Looking at Jacobsen, she said, "Sir, if I don't get out of this cabin and go do something, I will lose my mind." She surprised herself at the harsh tone, and immediately regretted saying anything. They were here to help, and needed her to work with them.

"I have an idea," said Marcus, standing.

"What is it?" Abbie asked.

"Dylan loves fire. We should build a campfire outside and see if it draws him. Can you do that, Hon? And I will go back to the woods and keep looking."

"No, I'm going with you!" she said, standing. Her intense gaze demanded agreement. "Don't think you can stop me."

"Look, someone needs to be here when he comes back. You're where he feels safest."

"That's why he needs me to be out there, finding him."

"One of us needs to be here, in case he comes looking for us. I'm a foot taller than you. I can cover more ground, faster."

A flood of guilt, shame and desperation welled up in her eyes. The sheer force of the emotions trying to escape began crumbling the dam she'd been using to hold them back. "But I can run," she begged as the dam crumbled. She dug her face into Marcus' shoulder to hide from the nightmare they were experiencing. Her sobs were audible, but muffled.

She felt his arms close around her in a grip so tight she could scarcely breathe. For the first time since they discovered Dylan's disappearance, she could feel just how scared he was. The tears hitting the top of her head confirmed how together they were in this.

"The fire actually sounds like a good idea, Abbie." said Jacobsen. "Anything that can attract his attention or help him want to come out of hiding would be helpful. Can you tell me about his other interests and fascinations? If he's wearing a life jacket, I assume he loves water."

Abbie came out from Marcus' shoulder, drew a deep breath and wiped her eyes. "He does, but he's only been swimming in a pool, so I don't know if he would connect that the lake is swimming water."

"He likely saw others swimming in it, though. We were trying to be proactive with the vest," said Marcus.

"We have officers posted at the shoreline and along the roadsides already. So, now we have water and fire. What else could draw him?"

"He was fascinated by the fireflies. We don't have them back home. I could see him following one into the woods," answered Marcus.

"And he loves dogs," said Abbie, "as long as they're not barking."

"Well, that gives us some good things to work with," Jacobsen replied, standing. "Abbie, are you willing to start the fire?"

Abbie nodded, her role no longer feeling secondary.

"Good. Marcus, do you know all of the people that are here?"

Marcus nodded.

"Then let's go out and get them ready to do an organized search."

Outside the cabin, Jacobsen climbed up on a picnic table and held up a lantern so he could be seen and heard. He looked at the crowd of faces, many who looked related. They were scared, and they needed a job to do.

"I am Trooper Jacobsen, from the Michigan State Police Department. Those of you willing to help search for Dylan, if you haven't checked in with Trooper Dunway right over there, please do so. This is important, as we need to make sure all searchers are accounted for.

"We need people who are healthy and vigorous. There are things you can do if you cannot walk ditches and woods and shoreline, so don't be discouraged if you have weak ankles or other health issues. It's going to take all of us to find him. For the walking part of the search, the terrain is much more rugged than one would think. Also, there is a K9 unit on the way. We will be making sure the searchers stay downwind from the dog so she can do her job without distractions. One more thing. Because of Dylan's sensitivities, this is the last loud announcement you will hear. From now on, we want to do our work as quietly as possible, so if he's hiding, we can make him want to come out."

Abbie listened carefully to the announcement as she crumpled up some paper she'd saved for kindling. The instructions brought up new fears. *What if Dylan had broken his ankle, or worse? The fire would be of no use then.* Once again, she wondered if she was just given a job to keep her occupied and out of the way.

"You know, if you make the paper balls looser, the air can get in to feed the flames," said her sister-in-law, sitting next to her.

Realizing she'd started smashing the paper instead of crumpling it, Abbie let out a small chuckle of agreement. "It's more of a sense of helplessness than anger," she said.

"I'm so worried. I can't even imagine what you're going through," Connie said softly. "Just so you know, you and Marcus are good parents. No one is blaming you for this."

"I am." Abbie stood the split wood on end in a teepee formation, then lit the paper. Staring at the flames as they caught the smaller wood pieces, she thought of how Dylan may have interpreted the happenings of the day. Her hope was that the amount of people here was just too much stimulation, and he went to find somewhere to hide. If that's what happened, the fire had a good chance of convincing him to come out of whatever hiding place he'd found. She desperately hoped that's where he was — somewhere quiet and safe.

Another police car showed up, this time a K9 Unit. *Odd how a dog can just show up and make a bad situation feel just a little better,* she thought. Overhearing the name, 'Officer Brownie' and assuming it was the name of the dog, she watched as Brownie's handler let her out and gave her a good sniff of Dylan's socks.

"Can I get you something to drink?" Connie asked, interrupting her train of thought.

Abbie didn't believe she deserve to be comfortable. How could she be when her son was lost in the dark, helpless? What kind of mother lets that happen? *No, you don't get coffee.* "No thanks," she answered.

"A cup of coffee would help you stay alert."

Abbie looked at Connie suspiciously, knowing she was being coerced into self-indulgence. She also knew the coercion was out of concern, and Connie needed a way to contribute. "Yeah, ok. Just black, though."

"I'm going to put Toby in bed, then I'll be back with your coffee." She picked up the grumpy-faced toddler and convinced him to drop the stick he'd found. "Come on, Sweet Cheeks, let's go sleepy!"

Sweet Cheeks was overtired, and made his disgruntled opinion known. The sound echoed through the night, as she carried him off to a nearby cabin.

A group of children old enough to have understanding of the situation was kept busy in one of the cabins, while the rest of the parents helped search. Those with very young children put them to bed.

By the time Connie returned with Abbie's freshly made coffee and a baby monitor, three other moms, two grandmas and one great-grandpa had joined them. "He'll turn up, Abbie, I just know it," one of them said.

"Maybe he got a little lost and decided to take a nap," said another.

The sound of footsteps and muffled voices joined the dance of flashlights and fireflies in the distance. Abbie jumped up and ran toward them. "Dylan?"

"We haven't found him yet," said Marcus. The despondency in his voice was evident as he added, "but we found this." He lowered his flashlight to let her see what was in his other hand. Marcus was holding a child's orange life jacket. Any hope that it was someone else's was lost when she saw the name "Dylan", written on the back in her own handwriting. Her thoughts erupted in a thousand micro calculations of swimming skills and drowning probabilities.

"This doesn't mean he's in the water," Marcus said flatly. "He's still out there, and we will find him."

She nodded, wanting to believe him. Her knees were not convinced. They buckled, dropping her to the ground. Her hands covered her face as the sobs filled them.

"I've got her, keep looking," Connie said to Marcus. She then knelt down in front of Abbie and offered her a shoulder to cry on.

"Thank you," Marcus replied, his voice cracking. "And Abbie..."

"Yes?"

"It's dry."

She threw her head back and looked toward the heavens, her hands raking her hair. "Let's just hope he is too."

Marcus started to close the gap between them, then stopped. "I've gotta keep looking, Abbie".

"Go," she said. "Find our boy."

As the group walked away, the flashlights disappeared into the night, becoming small enough to blend in with the glow of the fireflies that separated them. For the first time this weekend, Abbie paid attention to them. As each took their turn increasing and decreasing their light, she remembered what Marcus' pointed out. He *was fascinated by the fireflies.*

"Connie, would fireflies go toward the lake?" she asked.

"I don't know, but there is a breeze, so I would think they would stay among the trees and grasses."

Quickly, Abbie stood up. "I think so too. Let's get back by the fire."

Abbie was drinking her second cup of coffee when two men came out of the woods from the other direction, their flashlights bouncing through the trees on their way toward her. *They aren't coming for a break. Something's happened.*

She stood up, bracing herself for whatever news they would bring. Connie joined her.

"You're Abbie, right?"

"Yes".

"We found him. He appears to be just fine, but he's hiding under a bush. We didn't want to upset him, so Trooper Jacobsen sent us to get you. Deputy Dollanger here is going to take you to him. I'll go find your husband. The rest of you, please stay put."

The young Deputy took off toward the opposite side of the search area, not waiting for a reply.

Abbie's breaths were labored, her feet stuck.

"Follow me, Ma'am," Dollanger stated.

Abbie nodded. Why were her legs so heavy? She put one in front of the other, needing more focus than normal to walk. As the idea that her child was safe sank in, the weight of her legs lifted and she found herself nearly running. Dollanger's pace was quick, but intentional.

"Can we please go faster?" she asked.

"Sorry, Ma'am, but a twisted ankle won't get you there at all. Watch out for this branch." He pulled the branch back to allow her through.

If he weren't the only one who knew the way, she'd have left him behind and bolted. As it was, she could not be more grateful.

After what seemed like an eternity, they approached a small group quietly conversing. Jacobsen was there to greet her.

"Hello, Abbie, come with me. He's right over there. Just watch out for Officer Brownie. We had her stay with him, as she seems to be of comfort to him."

He walked a few yards over and pointed his flashlight to the German Shepherd laying quietly next to a bush, then handed her his light.

As she drew closer, she could see a familiar tiny hand holding Brownie's paw. His red shoe peeked out from another part of the bush. *He's ok — My baby's ok!* Abbie, though ecstatic, needed to see his face and to hold him for reassurance. She knew, however, that she would scare him if she reacted too quickly. She also knew it wouldn't be a good idea to startle the dog trained to find and protect him.

With perfect timing, Brownie's ears perked up and her head turned toward her handler. Immediately, she got up and left Abbie and Dylan to work out the rest.

"Good girl, Brownie." Abbie watched, both relieved and grateful as the dog walked past her.

The small group of officials behind her grew silent and watched as she spoke. "Dylan, Honey, Mama's been looking for you. Can you come out and give me a hug?" Her words were calm and peaceful, but inside she was in turmoil. She needed to hold him.

No longer holding the dog's paw, the small hand retracted into the bush.

Hurried steps came up behind her, nearly tripping to get to her. Abbie turned to see Marcus' approach.

"He's here!" she whispered.

Marcus nodded. His face held a firm expression, but the tears gave away his relief. His voice cracked as he spoke. "Hey, Dylan . . . Buddy . . . Would you like to come and see the fire? We can make some hot dogs. I'll bet Brownie has hot dogs sometimes. Maybe we can give her one too, if her dad says so."

"She's earned it," came a soft voice from behind them.

The bush rustled. No sooner had Dylan emerged from the bush than his parents embraced him. Dylan tried to reach for Brownie, but his arms were locked in place by his parents' embrace. "Pup...Pup...up," he said, rocking against their hold.

Abbie and Marcus looked at each other, then at him. Abbie spoke first. "Is he..?"

"I think so," Marcus answered. "Dylan, do you like the puppy?"

Dylan's face lit up, his grin nearly bigger than he was.

"Maybe we should think about getting him a dog," said Marcus.

At this point, Abbie was agreeable to nearly anything that would make Dylan happy.

The crowd near them began to grow, as word spread of Dylan's recovery. The growing number brought with them the sounds and sights of delight. An occasional effort to keep people quiet was heard, but the joy of finding him alive and safe was uncontainable.

"This is a lot for him. Too many people. Let's get him back to the cabin," Marcus told Abbie.

By lunchtime the next day, Abbie and Marcus had ordered a GPS watch, which was to be on their doorstep when they returned home. They also decided to leave a day early so they could relax in familiar surroundings after their ordeal. Accordingly, Marcus started loading the car while Abbie made lunch.

"Mac and cheese!?!" exclaimed Marcus, entering the cabin. "Dylan, are you eating mac and cheese without me?"

Dylan's face lit up with excitement as he put a spoonful in his mouth. The hot dog pieces remained in a separate bowl, waiting their turn.

"Yours is right here," said Abbie as she put it on the table.

"I want a bite of Dylan's. I'll bet his is better!" Marcus opened his mouth like a baby bird waiting to be fed.

Dylan obliged, enjoying this game. His scoop ended up with just one noodle hanging off the edge of the spoon, but it was enough. Marcus gulped it down like a big fish eating a minnow. To Dylan's delight, his dad exaggerated the act of chewing and swallowing, then smacked his lips. It was a lot for one noodle, but not too much for a dad eager to appreciate every moment.□

Names: Dylan, Abbie and Marcus□
From: Wausau
Highlight: Being found

The Guestbook

Ingrid, now 73, climbed the first step of the cabin's front porch slowly, the muscles in her right knee tightly protecting the joint. Remembering her mother's words, "There is no bad weather, only bad clothes," she stopped and tightened the twist of her scarf, tucking it back into her jacket. She sighed and grabbed the railing again.

Eleanora helped her with the second and last step, landing them on the porch. "Are you ready for this, Mom?" she asked, opening the door.

Ingrid gave a sheepish smile and stepped inside, stomping off her shoes by habit. The wet leaves from the earlier rainstorm remained stuck, as if glued.

"We're a bit early. Would you like some tea?" Eleanora asked, already on her way to the teapot.

"That would be nice, thank you." Ingrid slipped off her shoes and hung her fall jacket on the hook by the door, revealing the soft blue cardigan beneath. She took a deep breath and turned around, taking a mental note of each detail. In the early years of the resort, this cabin smelled like woodsmoke. Cleaning the ashes between guests was one of her more dreaded chores, as the ash seemed to get everywhere. When the propane insert was later added, she rejoiced. How much she missed that smell of a wood fire, though.

Her concentration was broken by Eleanora's question. "What's your best memory here?" she asked as she turned the burner on.

Ingrid scanned the decades for a favorite she felt she could share with her daughter. "I suppose it would be the day your father and I made that agreement with your grandfather. There has always been something about this cabin that I loved. I couldn't bear it to be destroyed."

"I, for one, am glad you saved it. There's so much history here. This was always my favorite to come and play in while you cleaned." Eleanora sat at the table and methodically opened the tea bags, adding one to each cup. As she slid a cup to Ingrid, she looked thoughtful. "Mom..."

"Yes?"

"Did we disappoint you by not taking over the resort?"

"Oh, no. This was our dream, not yours. You have your own lives to live."

"But that doesn't mean you aren't disappointed."

"Are you not happy where you are?"

Eleanora jumped up to catch the whistling teapot. She poured the boiling water over the teabags and put the kettle back on the burner to keep the water warm. "Oh, I am. But this place reminds me of Dad, and the thought of you having to part with it is a little hard for me." She pulled the string of the teabag, swishing it back and forth. "It's almost like losing a piece of him all over again."

"The resort will still be here, my dear."

Ingrid put her hand on her daughter's. Hers, of course, was more weathered, but the genes definitely had influence. There was a time when her hands were the younger, and her grandmother's the older. Time rolled on, picking up speed as the years went. She looked at their matching long fingers and wondered how many generations back the similar-looking hands went.

"I know, it's just . . . hard." Eleanora's words brought her back to the present.

"Your father would not have wanted this resort to be a burden placed on you. He would have wanted someone who loved it to buy it instead." Ingrid blew on her tea before taking a sip. The warm liquid chased away the last of the season's chill. Behind her, a buzzing sound came from the pocket of her jacket. Watching Eleanora jump up to hand her the phone, Ingrid asked her to answer it instead.

"Hello, this is Ingrid's phone. This is her daughter, Eleanora . . . yes, she's right here. We're at the cabin already, we were a bit.... oh, I see. How much longer, do you think? Ok, we'll see you then."

"Buyers or attorney?"

"Attorney. Apparently, there was a hang up with their court date this morning, but they'll be here in about fifteen minutes. The buyers will be with them. At least we have somewhere warm to wait. Would you like me to start the fireplace?"

"I'm good. The tea is warm enough, thank you."

"Did you ever find out how old this place was?"

"1923. It was built by a homesteader who then married a teacher. Do you remember the opera glasses?"

"Oh, that's right! The repair on the fireplace is hardly noticeable anymore. It seemed so obvious at first, but over time the mortar seems to have blended in. I'd completely forgotten about that."

"The stories these logs hold. If only we had a record of them," said Ingrid.

Eleanora topped off their tea with the rest of the hot water. As she went to sit again, the guestbook on the end table caught her eye. "Hey, I wonder if any of this would be interesting? I didn't realize you still had guestbooks in the cabins."

"Not in all of them, just this one."

"Really?"

Ingrid shrugged, offering no explanation.

Skimming through the book, Eleanora asked, "Any idea who this one was? From Marshfield, highlight is 'One very, very good dog'."

Ingrid thought for a moment, then gasped slightly. "That was a horrible night! If it weren't for that dog, who knows what would have happened?"

"I don't remember you telling me about this one."

"It was a warm night, breeze coming in through the windows . . . a good night for sleeping. That is, until this crazy dog started barking. We ignored it at first, but then we heard the man yelling the dog's name. Your father ran to see what was happening. The dog kept barking at the door of another cabin until the man staying there opened the door. The dog then ran past the man and laid down on the bed next to their little girl."

"Did he hurt her?"

"Turns out she was having a seizure. The dog just lay there and waited for them to figure it out. Your dad called 911."

"Are you kidding me? How did the dog know?"

"It turns out his previous owner was training other dogs to detect seizures. This dog must have learned right alongside them. Might have saved her life, we don't know."

"Wow,"

"If you think that's amazing, you should have seen the dog! Old English Bulldog. Wrinkled, sad-looking, arthritis in his hips. But that night, he was a hero."

"That's incredible. Which other ones stand out in here?" She skimmed some more. "How about this one? Miles and Rebecca, from Appleton. Highlight is the Elusive Kirtland's Warbler."

"Who are they?" Ingrid asked.

"I have no idea. I thought maybe local celebrities or something that I didn't know."

"Not that I know of. I don't remember anyone by those names. Perhaps they are birders."

"Ok, let's try this one. Sammy and Ben, from Escanaba. Their highlight is 'The kindness of strangers'. Did their car break down or something?"

Ingrid looked down into her coffee cup trying to remember a Sammy and a Ben. "I don't-wait, let me see the handwriting on that one."

"You'd remember the handwriting?"

"Well, if I was here cleaning, I'd have read them and remembered the guests." She tapped the page, her memory of the incident coming together. "This was that father and son trapped here in that awful blizzard. I told you about that one, I think."

"You did. Ever find out how that turned out?"

Ingrid nodded, smiling. "They made it to Rochester, and the boy turned out just fine. He was able to have a surgery that took care of his heart issues. The family stopped in that summer to meet us and pay for the door. Your father refused to let them."

Eleanora continued paging. Her gaze stopped on names she knew. "Mom, look at this!" She turned the book to show her mother as she read, "Aiden and Savannah (and either Johnathan Aiden or Jacqueline Eleanora), from Milwaukee. Highlight: New shoes." If John had been a girl, her middle name would have been Eleanora!"

"Can you blame them? You're a lovely woman and an excellent artist. I'm glad Savannah finally convinced you."

"I hadn't realized how many lives this place has touched."

"A lot of big decisions are made when people are on vacation. It gives people a chance to slow down and think. Sometimes, life throws us a curveball while we are traveling too." Ingrid put her cup up near her face, then paused. "Sometimes for good, sometimes for bad."

"Well, you and Dad have done a wonderful job running this place. It was a privilege to grow up here, too."

"I have loved being here. We did have a lot of fun, didn't we?"

The faint sound of closing car doors signaled the arrival of the new owners.

"It sounds like they're here," Eleanora said, heading for the door.

Ingrid stood as Eleanora ushered in the closing attorney and a middle-aged couple, full of the excitement of the next chapter in their lives. Their entrance brought in another blast of cold air. In response, Ingrid flipped the switch on the fireplace. "The fireplace will have the chill off in no time," she assured them.

As the room warmed, Ingrid braced herself for the finality of what was to come. Within minutes, papers were signed and the transition was complete. It happened so quickly, she could barely process that the transaction had been made.

Her thoughts fluttered to when she and Kristofer had just begun their journey with this place. Mattias' experience and skill made carpentry, plumbing and even electrical look simple. She and Kristofer quickly learned how little they knew, and they relied on her father's help a number of times to work through the process. She remembered fondly how her dear Papa talked to Kristofer like a son, never making him feel incapable of the job. The meals her mother and sister would bring as they worked late into the evening were lifesavers many times over. She could almost smell her mother's meatballs and lingonberry jam.

"You will always be welcome here, Ingrid. We would love to see you any time," said the wife, nodding her head in agreement with herself.

"Thank you, that is very kind. But I will be moving to Milwaukee with my Eleanora, and I don't know that I will be able to make the trip back much longer. If you don't mind, though, I would like to keep the guestbook, as a reminder of all that Kristofer and I have done here."

"Of course. Is there anything else here of sentimental value you'd like?" the husband asked.

"No, just the guestbook, thank you."

Sensing the lady needed a moment with the place, the husband stood up. "Well, we need to get these papers filed. It's been a pleasure to get to know you both." He offered his wife her coat and said, "If you'd like to take a last look around, please feel free. We'll be back later this afternoon."

"I appreciate that, thank you," said Ingrid. "It was nice to meet you as well. I am glad the place is in such good hands."

The three left as quickly, and with as much excitement, as when they'd come. Eleanora left her mother to peruse the guestbook as she cleaned and put away the dishes from their tea.

Ingrid paged through the guestbook slowly. Many names stood out in their repetition. These had become regular visitors and friends. There were two names, though, that she looked specifically to find. They were scattered throughout the book, with the last entry previously unread by her.

She smiled when she found it. Kristofer always signed the guestbook when they decided to stay there. Their last night in the cabin was just two weeks before his heart attack took him from her. He liked to make up names, but his handwriting was unmistakable. ☐

Names: Sven and Olga
From: New York City
Highlight: Olga

Ingrid closed the book and held it close to her. She started to tear up, but instead a large grin overtook her face. She quickly worked to remove it before her daughter turned around and asked. She barely succeeded.

"Would you like a moment, Mom? I can meet you in the car."

Ingrid walked toward the door and took her coat down from the hook. As she put her hand through the sleeves, she replied, "No, I'm ready". She took a deep breath and tied the belt of her jacket. The leaf pieces were now dried and slid easily from her shoes. Looking up at her daughter, she placed both hands over her heart and said, "All the *really* good stories are in here!"

Acknowledgements

As many an honest writer will tell you, no book has been written without the contributions of others.

Someone taught us to read, and instilled in us a love of the written word.

This would be my mom, Esther, who read to my sister and I nearly every night as children, and who encouraged us to become capable and confident women.

Someone gave us a love for the subject matter.

This would be my dad, Harlan, who passed down his love of time spent on the water by taking my sister and I water skiing — often.

Someone gave us the support we needed.

I am fortunate enough to have a supportive husband, Devon, who patiently brought me green iced tea and snacks when the story was flowing out of my fingers late into the night, unwilling to allow me to pause for sleep. His willing and eager support gave me the ability to take time away from work to pursue this endeavor, and I would have given up without him.□

I am also fortunate enough to have friends and family who have been of great support through the impostor syndrome and the anxiety, a common affliction to those writing their first book. This includes my Advanced Copy Readers, who were willing to give the honest feedback every author needs.

We needed experts.

My Editor and good friend, Kasha Stoll, leveled up my writing. Her honest, blunt and expert advice were invaluable, as each story became better than the last. The rewrites were worth the struggle, and I am confident that this is the best writing I have to give at this time. I look forward to many more cooperative works, if our lives allow that opportunity. □

Specialist Lieutenant Benjamin Eckola, of the Michigan State Police, was kind enough to offer me the information needed to make sure *Fireflies* would be believable. I am grateful not only for the information, but the work police and other organizations and individuals do to find and return lost children to their parents.□

My son, Michael, was kind enough to be a technical consultant, offering me a better prank for *The Elusive Kirtland's Warbler* than the original I came up with. His humor and insight were of great encouragement.

We needed community.

I would like to include as well, the real people and businesses mentioned in these stories, who allowed me to give a sense of place while mingling them in with the characters of my imagination. □

These include *Babycakes Muffin Company, Falling Rock Cafe, Jilbert's Dairy, Joe and Sons Service, the Marquette Regional History Center, and Miners Pasty Kitchen*. It has been a delight to get to know and work with you all.

We needed an imagination and the ability to share it.

Most importantly to me, I would like to thank the One who "Wonderfully made" us all, and who saw fit to give us each our natural abilities. I have enjoyed using what I was given to (hopefully) offer entertainment that can uplift and encourage, and appreciate the blessing this has been.□

We needed people to share our stories with.

To all of these who helped me get here, I would like to add my thanks to you, the readers, who have given me the opportunity to be a part of your lives and your imaginations, and for any online reviews you care to leave.

None of these kindnesses have been taken for granted.

Sincerely,

Deb

www.ingramcontent.com/pod-product-compliance
Lightning Source LLC
Chambersburg PA
CBHW050405110726
47899CB00008B/2657